Emma
catwalks
and
cupcakes!

SIMON SPOTLIGHT

An imprint of Simon & Schuster Children's Publishing Division

1230 Avenue of the Americas, New York, New York 10020

First Simon Spotlight paperback edition May 2018

Copyright © 2018 by Simon & Schuster, Inc.

All rights reserved, including the right of reproduction

in whole or in part in any form.

SIMON SPOTLIGHT and colophon are registered trademarks of

Simon & Schuster, Inc.

Text by Elizabeth Doyle Carey

Design and chapter header illustrations by Laura Roode

For information about special discounts for bulk purchases, please contact

Simon & Schuster Special Sales at 1-866-506-1949

or business@simonandschuster.com.

Manufactured in the United States of America 0418 OFF

2 4 6 8 10 9 7 5 3 1

ISBN 978-1-5344-1735-9 (pbk)

ISBN 978-1-5344-1736-6 (hc)

ISBN 978-1-5344-1737-3 (eBook)

Library of Congress Catalog Card Number 2018936049

CUPCAKE DIARIES

Emma
catwalks
and
cupcakes!

by coco simon

Simon Spotlight

New York   London   Toronto   Sydney   New Delhi

CHAPTER 1

The Audition

Yay! It's summer! And bummer! It's summer! I thought as my alarm chimed this morning at six thirty. It's always fun when the seasons change and I have a break from the regular school schedule, but summer also means more work for me. It still feels weird to say it, but it's really true: I'm a model.

Yup, me—good old Emma Taylor.

What started out as a small, occasional job at our local bridal store turned into a pretty good moneymaker for me and my family, so during the past year, I've gotten together a portfolio of professional photos of me in all different looks and styles (hair up, hair down, happy, dreamy, silly—you name it), and now I send out my one-sheet (usually an e-mail—with a few of my best photos, and my statistics: height, weight, hair and eye colors, skills, and contact information) and go on go-sees, which are like tryouts for models.

During the school year, I fit my modeling around my real life: school and sports and my best friends—Alexis Becker, Katie Brown, and Mia Vélaz-Cruz, plus our cupcake baking business, the Cupcake Club. But now that school was out for the summer, I'd be using all my free time to land modeling jobs and go on shoots.

My parents let me make all the decisions about it. Any job that I'm offered is mine to accept or decline. They think modeling is kind of weird, but they also like how the money I earn fattens my college fund. My mom had reluctantly fallen into the role of manager for my career (in addition to her job at the library), while my dad and sometimes my older brother, Sam, take me to jobs both near and far away.

Today was my first real day of summer vacation (yay!), but I had to head into the city for a go-see. My besties would be hanging out without me (bummer!), and I would not have a moment to relax.

The day started with an early alarm. Then I had to shower, clean my skin really well, double wash and condition my hair, take my vitamins, moisturize, and dry my straight blond hair perfectly, with just a little bit of a flip at the ends.

I do not usually wear makeup, but sometimes I use a lip shine and maybe a little bit of gel to hold my eyebrows in place. My mom is really uptight about me getting too into my looks, so she always checks my face to make sure I'm not wearing makeup. She thinks it's unhealthy for kids to have too many chemicals on their bodies (everything she buys for me to use is organic), and she also thinks I'm too young to wear makeup every day.

After I was all squeaky clean and fresh, I picked out my outfit according to what the memo was on the job I was going for. Today they were looking for girls for a winter coat ad (yes, it is June), and they wanted a wholesome and fresh look. Wholesome and fresh is my specialty! So I chose a plain, pale pink polo shirt; a new pair of dark blue jeans I'd been saving for a special occasion; and a pair of unscuffed pink sneakers with small white ped socks. I put a little pink clip in my hair to the side.

Downstairs, my mom was getting breakfast ready. She had the day off from the library, so she had time to drive me into the city.

"Hi, honey," she said. "And happy first day of summer!" She turned from the stove with a plate of scrambled eggs and buttered toast for me, plus a glass of my favorite juice: nectarine! Everything looked delicious.

"Thanks, Mama," I said, calling her my private, babyish name for her.

"I'm so impressed by how you get yourself up and get ready without any nudging from me," my mom said, crossing her arms and leaning back against the counter to study me. "When I was your age, I was so disorganized."

"Well, I like everything I do. I mean, I wouldn't do it if I didn't like it." I shrugged and then dug into my breakfast. As I was chewing, my phone pinged and I checked it. It was a text from Katie.

What's up, sister? Big plans for today? Let's celebrate summer together!

I sighed and put the phone down. Then I took another bite of toast and looked out the window. It was going to be a gorgeous June day. The perfect day to go to the lake, or to the town pool, or even to the mall with my friends. I felt a tiny bit sorry for myself for a second, but then I shook my head to clear it. Booking this go-see was my choice, and if I got this job, I'd make a really good amount

4

of money from it, like a quarter of a year's college tuition.

My mom was watching me, though. "What's the text?" she asked lightly. I could tell she didn't want to pry, but my facial expression must've given away my feelings. I sighed.

"It was Katie asking if I wanted to hang out and celebrate summer today. But that's okay. I can catch up with those guys later, anyway."

My mom nodded, studying me. Then she said, "Hey! Why don't you ask Katie to join us? I could take you girls for a quick lunch in the city, and we could stop by that cupcake place downtown that you've been wanting to check out."

I sat up straight in my chair, grinning. "Really? That would be so cool!"

Again, my mom nodded. "Sure! Ask her. And tell her that her mom can call me if she wants details, but we'll be home by four at the latest."

"Thanks, Mama!" My fingers flew over my phone's keyboard as I texted Katie back. I put the phone down, crossed my fingers and waved them at my mom, and then finished eating.

My phone pinged again, and I checked it.

Awesome! I'm in! What time should I be ready?

"Yahoo!" I cheered. My mom and I organized the details, and soon we were off.

At Katie's, she was standing outside on the sidewalk waiting for us.

"Wow, Emma!" Katie said as she closed the door of the minivan. "You look amazing! Like a real model!"

I laughed. "I guess I kind of *am* a real model now," I said.

Katie shook her head admiringly. "Your hair's all sleek and shiny, and your clothes are perfect, and your skin looks all dewy and fresh. I'd hire you if I were in charge, that's for sure!" She giggled. "I look like a mess next to you!"

I sized up Katie's bedhead and ripped jeans. She had on purple flip-flops and one of our old promotional cupcake T-shirts that was stained with what may have been strawberry extract.

"You look like you!" I said, squeezing her arm. "Adorable!"

Katie is naturally pretty, with wavy brown hair and friendly brown eyes. Her skin is fair, and she has a cute smattering of freckles across the bridge of her nose. If I were casting the role of "best friend" in a television show, I would pick her. Her fashion sense isn't the greatest, but she has other passions, and that's why I love her!

Katie looked down at my sneakers. "How do you keep everything so neat and perfect-looking all the time? If I even *see* chocolate, it stains me."

I had to laugh. It was true what she said. She was always a bit messy, and I am pretty careful when it comes to my clothes. I'm not prissy, but I take care of my things—probably because I know that it's hard to earn the money to pay for stuff, and also because I do need to look good to get jobs.

"Well, my jeans are new. I've been saving them for a special occasion. And the sneakers—I just wipe them down after I wear them. I have this little sneaker brush that I use. Also, I don't really wear them to the park or anything. These are definitely 'city sneakers.'"

"Wow," Katie marveled. "You have a lot of self-control."

"Not around cupcakes, though!" I laughed.

My mom interjected, "Speaking of which, what are Mia and Alexis up to today?"

Katie smiled. "Alexis starts her new job today. It's not really a job, though. It's part of a summer project at the town pool for Future Business Leaders of America, where she is learning about different opportunities in the food service industry."

"Wow, good for her!" said my mom.

Alexis is super career-minded. She's probably my actual best friend, because we've been close since we were toddlers, and our families are good friends. Katie and Mia are newer friends, and even though we're superclose, it's not like it is with Alexis and me. We can just read each other's minds. Sometimes that can be annoying, but mostly it's great.

"Yup. She says she wants to get a crash course in the food service industry, so she can decide if that's the area she wants to work in when she grows up. And Mia is taking a fashion design course at the community college and visiting fashion companies in the city for one day every other week," I said.

"Wonderful! And, Katie, sweetheart, what are you doing this summer?" she asked.

"Me? Oh. Not much. A cooking class at the high school for three weeks, then maybe day camp?" She winced. Day camp is a little babyish in theory, although the camp we all went to last year was awesome. It's just that the rest of us aren't going this summer.

"Fun!" Mom said.

Thinking about my friends' summers, I had mixed feelings.

I had to say I envied Alexis her very summery job. She would be at the pool and outdoors a lot. There would be tons of kids around all day, and maybe some cute boys. She was working in an industry that interested her. It was all good.

Mia was following her dream of becoming a fashion designer.

And Katie . . . Well, Katie was keeping it casual, which was also cool.

I'd be pretty busy, working a lot, in and out of the city. It was hard and a little lonely, and definitely not that summery!

"Mom, by the way, what's the deal with shooting winter coats in June?"

My mom laughed and looked at me in the rearview mirror. "I cannot pretend to understand the fashion industry, my dear. All I know is they have very long lead times for magazines, which means they need photos months in advance. The online ads go up much faster, though."

Katie looked at me, her eyes wide. "Wait, you're going to be putting on winter coats today?"

I had to giggle at the look on her face. "Yeah. Crazy, right?" I shrugged.

"And you have to pretend like you're not sweltering in them?"

I nodded. "Modeling can be a little like acting sometimes."

My mom chimed in. "A lot of the time when you're looking at a model on the beach, all bundled up, it's actually July and eighty-five degrees—in the shade!"

"That's nuts!" Katie laughed. "No wonder they pay you the big bucks!"

Soon, we reached the city, and my mom dropped us off outside the studio building.

"I'm going to look for parking. If you don't see me up there, just call me when you're finished, and I'll come with the car, and we'll drive to lunch, okay?"

I knew the drill, so I wasn't nervous to go on my own without her. "Thanks. No problem," I agreed. I gathered my portfolio and took one last peek in the side mirror, and then we headed in.

This is the part where I always start to get a little anxious. Katie and I got into the elevator with two other girls and their moms. The moms smiled stiffly at me (I guess we're all in competition), but the girls didn't smile at all. They just flicked their eyes up and down over me and Katie, quickly sizing us up.

When the elevator doors opened with a *ping*, Katie and I followed the quick-stepping moms and their little models to a central desk in a massive waiting area. I kept my eyes trained on the receptionist because if I start looking at everyone else, I get really nervous.

The competition at these things is always really, really impressive, but I've learned to stay inside my own head and not worry about other people. Just because there are some really beautiful girls at a go-see, it doesn't mean they'll get the job over me. The advertisers usually have a look in mind, and it's not always about who's the prettiest or tallest or whatever.

When we got to the front of the line, the receptionist gave me a clipboard, and I signed in. Then I said, "Would it be okay if my friend Katie joins me when I'm called? She's just an observer, but I thought it would be fun for her to see what goes on at an audition."

"Sure, honey. No problem. Just explain to the folks inside and make sure she stays off to the side so she doesn't distract anyone, okay?"

"Thanks. Will do," I agreed.

Katie and I looked for a place to sit and wound up standing by the door, almost in the hall. I knew it would take a while though, so we slid down the wall to sit and wait.

Katie giggled. "Emma, all these girls look just like you!"

I dared to take a quick survey and then turned back to her. "Not really. They have different hair colors and outfits, and some are taller. . . ."

Katie waved her hand impatiently. "No, but they're all superpretty and clean and neat and kind of sporty-looking, like you."

"Oh. Yeah." I had to agree. "That was the brief—the memo they put out on what they were looking for: sporty, fresh, clean, and casual. That's why everyone looks the same."

"Huh," said Katie, grinning as she continued to stare at everyone.

"Stop staring," I whispered.

It was fun having her there to lighten things up and remind me how crazy this all is. Despite everything I say about not caring about modeling and whatever, I kind of do. I mean, I always want to get picked, and I do get bummed when I don't make the cut.

"Emma Taylor?" someone called, and I popped up and smoothed my hair.

Katie popped up too.

"Let's do this!" I said, holding up my hand for a high five.

"We're going to kill it in there!" she said, smacking my palm enthusiastically.

Little did I know how true it would be when she said "we."

CHAPTER 2

Getting Picked

*H*eading into the darkened room was really intimidating, but Katie grabbed my hand and squeezed it, and I felt better. It was so great to have a friend with me today. Besides entertaining me, she had calmed me down. I introduced her to our escort, and when we reached the table of advertising people and art directors, the escort nicely introduced both of us.

"Team, this is Emma Taylor. You'll have her sheets right on top there, and you can see she's done a lot of bridal, and some local media, as well as two nationals. Accompanying her today is her friend Katie Brown, a civilian." Everyone laughed at that last part.

I swallowed hard and smiled. "Hello, I'm Emma,"

I said, and gave a little wave to the men and women sitting at the long table. They smiled back, friendly.

"Are you ready to try on some cozy, warm coats on this brisk winter day?" joked one of the sales representatives, handing me a pale blue wool pea-coat and a bright yellow scarf.

"Yes, I'm freezing!" I joked back as I took the clothes from her, and they all laughed.

Katie laughed too, and all the adults seemed to suddenly remember she was there. They turned to look at her, and I cringed a little. Maybe it was too disruptive to bring a friend on a job. Maybe I shouldn't have—

"What's your name again, dear?" asked one of the marketing representatives. She cocked her head as she looked at Katie.

"Oh, I'm Katie. I'm just Emma's friend—along for the ride today."

I noticed that everyone was now looking at Katie as I tightened the scarf around my neck.

"So natural and lovely," another sales representative whispered.

I glanced at her and realized she was describing Katie and not me.

"I love her hair," agreed the other lady. "Beautiful texture and waves."

One of the men overheard them and chimed in, more loudly, "She definitely has a fresh, new look."

Then the other woman said, "She looks free and beautiful. . . . No slave to fashion here! The ripped jeans, the casual flip-flops . . . somehow it all works."

Meanwhile, I was starting to sweat in my wool outfit. I cleared my throat.

The first lady glanced at me. "Very nice, Emma." But then she turned back to Katie.

What is happening?

Katie was standing frozen in place off to the side. I think she realized what was going on before I did.

"Katie, have you ever done any modeling before?" asked one of the men.

Katie gulped and laughed at the same time. (How she managed that—I don't know.) "Model? *Me?*" she said. "No . . . not . . . honestly, never."

One of the women went over to the coatrack and began flipping briskly through the coats. "What's your favorite color, Katie?" she asked.

Katie shrugged. "I don't really have a favorite," she said. "When people ask me that question I usually say rainbow! But if I had to just pick one . . . purple, I guess."

The woman handed Katie a long purple winter

16

coat and a white scarf. "Would you mind putting this on for a moment and letting us see how you look?"

Katie and I exchanged a quick glance. It was as if she was looking to me for permission, but it wasn't like it was up to me!

I gave her a little shrug as if to say *Whatever*, and so Katie put on the coat. The woman fluffed Katie's hair and then stepped back to admire her work.

"Delightful!" the first man said.

"So much fun!" the second woman agreed.

"I love this new direction," the second man said.

The woman looked over at me, still standing there awkwardly in the peacoat. "Emma, dear, you can take that off and just relax for a moment," she said. Then she turned back to Katie. "Katie, would you or your parents have any objection to you modeling our coats?" she asked.

Katie was at a loss for words. "I honestly don't know," she said. "I would have to ask my mom about it. I really never thought about modeling before."

"Oh, I'm sure you'd love it!" one of the women chirped. "Why, just ask your friend Emma here!" She turned to me with a bright smile. "Don't you love modeling, Emma?"

I was at a loss for words too. But what could

I do? I took a deep breath and tried to regain my composure. "Oh definitely," I said. I even managed a weak smile. "You would have fun, Katie," I said.

Katie looked at me, unsure.

"Then it's settled," the marketing representative said. (She was the one who first noticed Katie and asked her name.) She picked up the phone and called the receptionist. "You can send the rest of the girls home. We've made our selection. Please bring in the paperwork."

I hung the peacoat and scarf back on the rack and picked up my portfolio. I wasn't sure if I should leave or stay, so I just kind of stood there.

A moment later the receptionist came back into the room. "Congratulations, Emma," she said.

"Oh, no, our new model is Katie," one of the men interjected. "Could you please set her up with all the necessary paperwork?"

"Of course!" the receptionist said, not missing a beat. She turned her big grin on Katie. "Well, Katie! It looks like you've been discovered!" she said. "How does it feel?"

Katie looked back at me and then at the receptionist again. "It feels . . . confusing. But also a little exciting, I guess."

The receptionist took Katie gently by the arm.

"Please come by my desk, dear," she said. "I need some information from you, and there are some forms to take home for your parents."

The men and women sitting in the room stood up to leave, but then they suddenly realized that I was still standing there like a dope.

"Oh, Emma, you're lovely," one of the women said. "But I'm sure you already know that! We'll keep you in mind for future assignments."

"Absolutely," one of the men agreed. "But you must be so excited for your friend!"

"Oh, I am . . . ," I began. They all looked at me expectantly, but I couldn't think of anything else to say, so we all walked out.

Downstairs, Katie and I waited outside the building for my mom. I was so dumbfounded by what had just happened that I couldn't even think of a thing to say.

After a minute or two, Katie said, "So . . . *that* was a surprise."

I had to laugh. "Yeah, it was." I was glad she had broken the ice.

"Are you upset that they offered me the job and not you?" Katie asked. She turned to look at me, her brown eyes large and serious. "I feel really bad."

"No, of course not," I said. "Don't feel bad. These things happen all the time. Anyway, I think it's great you're getting a chance to model. I'm just a little taken aback, that's all." It took a lot of effort to be kind right then.

"Oh good," Katie said. I could see she was relieved. "I'm glad."

Right then my mom rolled up, and we climbed in. We were both silent.

"How did it go?" Mom asked as we buckled up.

"Great!" I said, mustering as cheery a voice as possible.

"Oh, sweetie, that's wonderful. When do you start?"

"Um, I don't," I said. "But *Katie* does!"

My mom eased the car into a bus lane, put the car in park, and turned around. "Did you say *'Katie'*?" she asked. I nodded. My mom couldn't hide her surprise.

"Why, Katie . . . that's—that's wonderful," she stammered. I could see her giving Katie a quick once-over. Her eyes lingered on Katie's wrinkled and stained T-shirt and faded flip-flops, and I cringed inwardly, thinking of the moms in the elevator earlier. Had my mom turned into one of them? Had I turned into one of those girls? Would life be a lot simpler and more fun if I were working at the town pool this summer?

"I'm sorry, dear. I don't mean to act so surprised. It's just that you . . . you're . . ."

"Not really the model type?" Katie said cheerfully. "I know! Nobody was more surprised than me! This whole thing is so weird. I'm not sure my mom will even let me do it. I mean, nothing personal . . ."

I waved my hand. I knew she didn't mean anything bad by it.

"It's just that with her dental practice being so busy now that school is out, she really doesn't have time to take me into the city for these sorts of things, so . . ."

"Well . . ." My mom looked at me and then at Katie and then back at me again. "It certainly is a surprise."

"I'm starving!" I said, changing the subject. "Where are we going for lunch?"

The rest of the day was fun. I put the awkward modeling thing out of my mind and enjoyed our lunch at this cool, open-air taco stand downtown. Katie and I chowed down on an assorted taco platter with all kinds of fillings: shredded pork carnitas, stewed lamb birria, pulled chicken, and more. We were so full and had so much fun. Everything was back to normal for a bit.

The Three Sisters cupcake store was tucked on a cute little cobblestone side street, with tiny boutiques and chic cafés everywhere. We spotted the pink-and-white–striped awning from up the block and speed walked up to it.

Katie had first seen it on a cooking show, *Exclusive Sweetshops Worldwide* or something, and she'd DVRed it so we could all watch it the next time the Cupcake Club met at her house. As soon as we saw the episode, we swooned over the store, agreeing that if the Cupcake Club ever opened its own shop, it would be just like this one.

It was owned by (surprise!) three sisters, and it was very girlie inside, decorated with lots of pink and white and floral patterns and stripes, and white marble–topped tables with chairs that had gold curlicued backs and pink leather seats.

The cupcake flavors were awesome, from Primrose (pink vanilla cake with pale pink, rose-flavored frosting, and tiny candied rose petals on top) to Sleepover Party (dark fudgy cake with a cookie dough center, and salted caramel frosting studded with marshmallows and a sprinkling of crushed potato chips). It was pure heaven!

My mom had given us money and told us to pick out eight cupcakes—two for each member of the club, all different—and one of the sisters boxed them for us in a pink-and-white–striped bakery box with a big pink bow. I couldn't wait to show Mia and Alexis, so Katie texted them to meet us at my house in about two hours. We took tons of photos of every detail to put up on social media with the hashtag "#cupcakecrushing," including a couple of selfies.

As we turned to leave, the sister behind the counter said to me, "Hey! Don't I know you from somewhere?"

"Me?" I asked in surprise. "Um, maybe?"

"Are you a model?" she asked.

"Well, yes. I mean, I do some modeling. Maybe you've seen some of my ads."

"I'm sure! You did the She's So Lovely campaign for The Special Day, right?" She was smiling and pointing her finger at me. "Gotcha!" she said with a grin.

I laughed. "Yes."

"I'm a model too!" Katie piped up.

Inwardly, I winced, since it wasn't the coolest thing to brag about and also because, come on—she was barely a model, but I didn't say anything.

"Could I get your card, or your sheet, or whatever, please?" the sister asked me. "We're about to do a big campaign to target teenage girls for cooking classes and birthday parties, and we need a face. You'd be perfect!"

"Wow! Sure. Thank you so much! I have one in the car up the street. Or, you know what? I can just e-mail my information to you. Or you can contact my agent."

"Great. I'm Lindsay Miller, by the way." She put out her hand, and I shook it.

"Emma Taylor. Nice to meet you. I love your store! We've been watching your *Exclusive Sweetshops Worldwide* episode on repeat."

Lindsay busied herself getting me her business card. "Are you girls huge cupcake lovers?"

Katie and I explained the Cupcake Club to her, and Lindsay said, "Wow! Now we really need to hire you. You're the real deal. Send me your info, and we'll be in touch, okay?"

Katie piped up, "I'm sorry I can't send you mine because I don't have it yet, but if I get it together, I'll send mine too."

It was a little awkward because Lindsay hadn't actually been asking Katie for her information.

24

Plus, it kind of annoyed me that Katie was butting in like this.

Today would definitely be the last time I would ever bring a friend on a go-see. Talk about a bad idea.

"Okay, thanks, girls!" said Lindsay, waving as we left.

We both waved back at her.

"Wow! That was so cool that she recognized you!" Katie said when we got outside. "You're like . . . a celebrity!"

I had to admit, I was pretty psyched, but I didn't want to let on, so I said, "Yeah. That was pretty cool."

"Does that happen to you a lot?"

"No, not really. I mean, maybe locally, like in town, but in the city? Never."

Katie chattered on. "Are you psyched to work for them? You know the first thing Alexis will want to know is if we can do a collaboration with them or some kind of cross-promotion, right?"

"Oh wow! I didn't even think of it! Just wait until she gets her marketing wheels spinning. Watch out!"

We laughed, and the stress of the day floated away again as we began chatting about cupcake business. I was looking forward to seeing Mia and Alexis when we got home and hearing all about Alexis's first day at her pool project. I was sure it had been awesome. Plus it would be a relief to talk about something—anything!—besides Katie's new modeling career.

CHAPTER 3

Career Surprises

Wait, start over again from the part in the elevator!" Mia was saying as we waited for Alexis to arrive. We were hanging out at the kitchen table at my house, rehashing our day.

Katie laughed and began retelling the day's adventures from basically the beginning. For the third time.

I couldn't help myself. I sighed and maybe even rolled my eyes the tiniest bit.

My mom and dad had been very reluctant to let me start modeling, back when I first began. They cautioned me about how phony the industry was and how it places value on the wrong aspects of a person—things you can't even control (like height) or develop through practice. They warned me that

I would have my feelings hurt repeatedly in the line of duty. Overall, now that I'd been in it for a while, I agreed with them, and I was glad they had taken the time to educate me about all this before I started.

But the truth was, I *do* enjoy it. I've worked with some really fun people (especially my friend Mona, who owns the local bridal salon—she "discovered" me), and I've had some cool experiences (meeting the mega–movie star Romaine Ford, for one). I've made great money, and I know I've gained confidence from it all. Yes, of course, as with anything, there are downsides. But for the most part, I do think modeling is a decent job.

The one thing my family—my parents and my three brothers—is very big on is not letting any of it go to my head. If I come home from a job and I still have on makeup, my brothers make fun of me and my parents make me rush to take it off. If my mother catches me mentioning anything negative about my looks or my body, she warns me that I might have just done my last modeling gig. And heaven forbid I say anything that sounds like bragging. They'll jump all over me the second it's out of my mouth.

Obviously, Katie's mom hadn't had a chance to

talk to her about any of this—she wouldn't even know what was going on until Katie got home and told her!—but her bragging attitude was creeping back in. If I had to hear her say one more time about how I had been "all dolled up for the job" and she "rolled out of bed and got it," well, there was no saying what I'd do!

Luckily, Alexis walked into my house right then. We'd been waiting for her to finish her shift at the pool, and I for one couldn't wait to hear all about it.

She was learning more about a business she's interested in. Plus, she gets to go into the pool on her breaks, and she sees tons of kids we know from school. She'll be up to speed on all the news around town, and she'll probably see some cute boys and get to eat ice cream every day. It just sounds like lots of fun. Like a real, old-fashioned summer.

Hmm . . . but maybe not.

Alexis dropped her bag in our mudroom and beelined through the kitchen to the couch in the family room. "I've had a *day*!" she said dramatically as she flopped onto her back on the sofa and flung an arm over her eyes to shield them from the light overhead.

We scurried in after her and perched on various seats around the room.

"What's up, Alexis?" I asked from the beanbag chair on the floor. "How did it go? I'm dying for details!"

"It was awful! Just awful!" Alexis said with a shudder.

"What?" I sat upright and exchanged worried looks with Mia and Katie. Alexis had been so psyched for this project. What could possibly have gone wrong?

"What on Earth happened?" said Mia, reaching over and rubbing Alexis's arm in concern.

Alexis strongly dislikes being "pawed," as she calls it. Mia always forgets that. Alexis flung off Mia's hand and sat bolt upright.

"My boss is a menace!" she said, and she flopped back dramatically.

We looked at one another in concern.

"Who's your boss?" asked Katie.

"Mary Jane Parks. And she's the meanest, pickiest, bossiest boss who ever bossed!"

I had to crack a smile at Alexis's description. "Why?"

"'Alexis, the ketchup labels need to face out!' 'Alexis, don't give out so many napkins!' 'Alexis, you're not using enough ice in the sodas!'" she mimicked. "Ugh!"

"Was there anything you did right?" Mia asked hopefully.

"Apparently not," Alexis said grimly.

"How old is this Mary Jane person?" I asked. Maybe she was a cranky old lady who was annoyed at having a kid work for her?

"Fifteen," Alexis sighed.

"Fifteen!" shrieked Mia. "Seriously?"

"Why is she so bossy?" I asked. My mental image of Mary Jane Parks was now completely revised.

"She's been there for three years already, and Mrs. Chilson—she's the real boss—loves her. Just *loves* her! It's 'Oh, Mary Jane this,' and 'Mary Jane that,' and 'Mary Jane prefers it when X, Y, and Z.' But Mary Jane's awful. She's mean!" Alexis huffed and folded her arms across her chest.

"Well, how's the job otherwise?" asked Katie.

Alexis inhaled deeply. "It's fine. I mean, it's fun to be there because it's so busy and summery and you see everyone. And you're kind of looked up to by all the little kids. They come around begging for free cups of sprinkles and stuff. . . ."

"Which I am sure you do not give them?" I said. Alexis is all about the bottom line—getting her to give discounts or give away free stuff in our cupcake business is nearly impossible.

"Absolutely not!" said Alexis.

"Phew! We wouldn't want you to compromise your business principles just for a job," I teased.

"The cleaning up is a bummer. Kids spill like two milkshakes an hour, and there are lots of bees because of all the spilled soda. It's pretty greasy inside the snack bar. Luckily, I don't have to do any cooking. I'm not licensed to work the Fry-o-lator. . . ."

"Thank goodness!" said Mia, laughing.

"But I *do* have to wear a hairnet and plastic gloves. . . ."

We smiled at the mental image of that.

Let me tell you, modeling was starting to look like a walk in the park compared to Alexis's summer project.

"Listen, I think we should all come by tomorrow and scope out this Mary Jane person and watch you in action!" I suggested.

Everyone readily agreed, and we set the time for noon the next day. Then we unpacked the Three Sisters cupcakes and laid them out on a big cutting board with a sharp knife. This is how we like to do our tastings: We cut each cupcake into quarters by making an X through it from top to bottom. Then we each take a plate and load up our cupcake

32

quarters and taste each flavor at the same time so we can discuss it. Katie keeps a tally on a piece of paper of which ones we like best. We score them from one to ten.

"Okay, first up . . . Strawberry Cheesecake!" directed Mia.

We each lifted the yellow-and-red–swirled cupcake and brought it to our mouths at the same time.

"Go!" said Katie, and we each took a bite.

"Mmm. Creamy!" said Alexis.

"I like that the strawberry is tart!" Mia said thoughtfully. "I wasn't expecting that. It's like strawberries with cream but unsweetened."

I wrinkled my nose. "Not my favorite," I said.

"It tastes authentic. I'll give them that. But it's more of a cupcake for grown-ups," said Katie.

I rated it a three, Mia and Katie both gave it a five, but Alexis was more generous. She gave it a seven, but then again she likes unsweetened stuff since her mom is super into health food.

Sleepover Party was next (I picked it because I'd had my eye on it from the start), and it was insanely delicious. The burst of chewy cookie dough in the center was a winner, and the salty caramel frosting and potato chip topping was a great contrast to the sweetness of the cake. We all gave it a nine and agreed it would be the main event of any sleepover party.

A few others were just so-so until we got to cupcake number seven, A Summer Day.

"What do you think this one is?" asked Mia, lifting her quarter and looking at it from all angles.

"I have no idea," I said. "I'm going for it!"

"One, two, three!" Alexis counted us in, and we took a bite.

"Oh wow!" I closed my eyes and tipped my head back. "Mmmmm!"

"Okay, this is *delicious*! Like, seriously delicious!" agreed Mia.

"What's in it, Katie?" Alexis asked. We always turn to Katie for cooking and flavor info since she's the chef among us.

Katie closed her eyes and chewed, then swallowed and paused. "Okay. The cake itself is cotton candy. For sure. That is really unique, and we've got to do that in our next test baking session. The frosting is . . . would you all agree it tastes just like vanilla soft-serve ice cream? The sprinkles on top would confirm that, and the pointy swirl from the frosting application. It's like a summer day at the snack bar!" said Katie with a laugh. "Right, Alexis?"

"Harrumph!" said Alexis. "I thought I liked it up until you said that."

"Poor Alexis!" I said, devouring the second part of my cupcake. I wished we'd gotten more and was already trying to think of when I'd be back in the city to go to Three Sisters again. "I'll get more, and we won't let Mary Jane Peterson have any!"

"It's Mary Jane Parks!" snarled Alexis.

"Sorry!" I said. "I didn't know you cared!"

Alexis stormed back to the family room to watch one of her endless dance competition reality shows while the rest of us tried the last cupcake and then cleaned up.

Katie was already on her phone, checking how to make cotton candy–flavored cupcakes.

"Poor Alexis," Mia said quietly. "She was so psyched for that job and looking forward to learning so much about the food service industry. I feel so bad for her."

"Yeah," I agreed. "Maybe when we go there tomorrow, we can lighten things up or even try to think up some ways for her to make it better."

"She could always quit," said Katie, her fingers flying over her phone.

"Alexis? Quit? Ha!" I laughed. "Have you met Alexis Becker?"

Katie looked up and smiled at me. "Good point."

"We'll think of something," said Mia.

✿

After the cleanup we were all hanging out in the family room, watching Alexis's show, when the topic of Katie's modeling job came up. Alexis hadn't heard the details so now I had to live through it all *again* for the umpteenth time.

I have to say, I was really sick of it at this point. The more I thought about how I'd encouraged Katie to come and she'd then stolen my job out from under me, the madder I got. (Of course I was conveniently forgetting that the job could have gone to one of any of the dozens of girls who were there with us.)

"I think it's superamazing!" Alexis squealed. "Katie, just think—you were 'discovered' today! This could be the start of a very successful career for you!"

"Katie Brown, America's next top model. Who knew?" Mia joked.

"Who knew?" I muttered. "Who knew that messy hair and dirty clothes would be just the look they were after?"

I knew it was mean, and I hadn't really meant to say it out loud, but I was kind of glad I had. I'd been feeling like saying something about Katie's "style" all day.

But then everyone turned and stared at me.

I forced a little laugh. "Oh come on!" I said. "Katie, don't feel bad. I'm sorry. I'm just being honest. It's just . . . look at you!"

I could see that Katie was, unfortunately, hurt.

"I thought you didn't mind my modeling," she said finally.

I was sorry I'd said what I was thinking, but I wasn't sorry I was thinking it, which made it hard to apologize. I may have gone too far, but I was frustrated.

"Katie, I didn't mean to hurt your feelings," I said. "Honestly, I didn't. But you have to understand where I'm coming from. I took so long to get ready for that go-see. And then you . . . you just basically roll out of bed and get the job? Seriously. It's just not fair. Not really."

"Modeling agencies are always searching for 'new looks,'" Mia pointed out. "Who knows? Katie may be the next big thing."

I rolled my eyes. *I hope not,* I thought.

"Look," said Alexis. "It's a bummer you didn't get the job, Emma. I know your modeling go-sees are something you work hard on and that it's disappointing when you don't get the job." She looked at me kindly. "But it's great that Katie did, if the contract had to go to anyone else. Jobs come and go, but friends last forever, right?"

I sighed. "Yeah. I guess."

Alexis continued, "You know something good will come out of today, so don't worry. Katie's thing might just be a fluke or it might be the beginning of a big career. But it's unlikely you two will ever be competing for the same job again. You have such different looks." She shrugged. "Okay? Peace?"

"Okay." I choked out an apology that I knew was right but that I didn't really feel yet. "Sorry, Katie."

"I'm sorry too, Emma. I never set out to take work from you."

I sighed again. "I know."

"I might even hate it," said Katie.

Privately, I hoped so, which was awful. I had to let my annoyance go, but I didn't really feel better.

After the Cupcakers had left and we'd confirmed our plan to meet at the pool the next day, my mom came into my room to chat.

"Everything okay?" she asked, sitting down next to me on my bed.

I groaned because everything wasn't okay. I'd been wanting to talk to her all day about what had happened, but there'd always been someone else around. I was glad she came to check on me.

"I feel like such a jerk for having such bad feelings," I admitted.

"You're talking about what happened with the job in the city this morning?"

I nodded. "I guess I'm . . . jealous, maybe? And mad. Just plain mad. Like, I invite my friend to do something fun, something that's mine, and she steals it out from under me. I just feel so mad!"

"I know. I understand," said my mom. She bit her lip and thought for a minute. "You know how Dad and I feel about the modeling business. For an industry that's so focused on beauty, it brings out some ugly feelings in lots of different ways. It's okay to feel mad, but you can't blame Katie. She certainly didn't set out to have that happen. You can be mad at the people who picked her if you want, but don't be mad at Katie."

"Still mad," I muttered, and my mom laughed.

"It will fade," she said. "Just focus on the things you love to do with your friends. It's summer! And remember, the fashion world is always changing. Who knows what will be in tomorrow? It might be that everyone wants redheads, and suddenly, Alexis is in high demand!" She tickled me until I smiled.

"I guess."

"Any fun plans?" she asked, and I told her about our arrangement to meet at the pool the next day.

"Good," she said. "Have fun and just relax. You can always find another job, but it's not as easy to find another friend. And anyway, at your age, summer should be about fun and not work. Not quite yet. So enjoy it while you can."

She hugged me good night and left me with my summer reading, which I'd promised myself I'd get out of the way ASAP this summer (which is what I promise myself every summer, and it never happens!).

I made up my mind to forget all about work and just enjoy the summer for a few days.

CHAPTER 4

Pool Time

Mia's stepbrother, Dan, drove Mia, Katie, and me to the town pool the next day. He's nice, even if he is majorly into heavy metal music and kind of goth stuff. Today, Dan was meeting a friend at the pool for a swim and then was heading out to his job. Mia's mom would pick us up at the end of the afternoon.

We checked in at the entrance, and then we piled through the gate to try to claim some lounge chairs together. Unfortunately, they were all taken, at least for now, so we grabbed a lunch table near the snack bar—waving all over the place at kids from school—and hoped that some lounge chairs would be free after lunch when the moms went home with the little kids for naptime.

The whole complex was crowded. There were kids of every age, shooting basketball at the outdoor courts, playing four square or hopscotch, fooling around on the swings, and of course, swimming in the pool. The pool itself was really made up of three pools. There was a diving pool that was really deep, a regular pool that was pretty shallow (only seven feet deep in the deep end), and then a baby pool that had a gradual entrance, like the ocean, which got deeper inch by inch until it was two feet deep. There was also a sprinkler area outside the pools, with posts of various heights spraying out water in different ways: streams, mists, and geysers. There was something for everyone, and today's clear skies and warm temperature were the perfect weather for enjoying it all.

To secure a lunch table and chairs, we draped our towels over them to save our spots. Then the three of us took our money and joined the long line for the snack bar. We could see Alexis hustling around behind the counter, and we giggled a little at her hairnet, but it didn't look too bad. There was a guy—an adult—working in the back (he must have been Fry-o-lator–certified) and a young boy who seemed to be doing a lot of heavy lifting—bringing in cases of soda and taking out the trash—and then there was a very petite dark-haired girl who was standing inside doing nothing, her arms folded across her chest and a look of total boredom on her face.

I wondered aloud what her role might be.

"Maybe she's with the health department," joked Mia. "She makes sure no one forgets to wash their hands after they go to the bathroom!"

"No wonder she looks so bored," Katie said with a laugh. "How many times a day could people need to go to the bathroom?"

"Oh, maybe she does inventory control and she has to count sprinkles. That could be why she looks so bored!" I kidded.

We inched forward, and the smell of French fries and grilled meat filled the air. My stomach rumbled as kids jostled for positions at the front of the counter.

Alexis saw us and waved, but stayed very professional, writing down orders and calling them in to the guy in the back. She scooped ice cream into tall silver canisters and set them to run on the milkshake machine while she bustled around assembling orders. The other girl seemed to do nothing except occasionally glare at Alexis. It was weird. Alexis obviously could have used the help, and the young boy seemed to pitch in as needed, but it was a lot of work.

Finally, we reached the front.

Alexis grimaced at us in some version of a smile, but she didn't have time for any small talk.

We placed our orders, and then I asked quietly, "Where's you-know-who?"

Alexis jerked her head toward the bored snack bar girl, and my eyes widened.

"She's your boss?" I asked incredulously. "*That's* Mary Jane?"

Alexis nodded and rolled her eyes.

"But she isn't *doing* anything!" I whispered.

Alexis shrugged. "She's critiquing my every move and will report it back to her boss, Mrs. Chilson, when I go on break," she whispered back.

"Wow," I said, and then I explained to the others.

We all took a good look at Miss Mary Jane Parks, and when we reached our lunch table to await our number to be called, we decided we needed to act.

"We need to plot revenge!" said Mia, her eyes blazing.

"But it should be devious. Something not too obvious!" agreed Katie.

I thought for a minute. "You know how Alexis

always has her mottoes? What's that one about winning bees with honey?"

"You catch more bees with honey?" said Mia. "Something about being nice to mean people?"

I pointed at her. "That's the one. What if the Cupcake Club made some delicious cupcakes for Alexis to bring in for the staff, as a morale booster?"

"I like it!" said Mia, nodding.

"Let's do it! Sweeten her up!" agreed Katie.

"We bake tonight!" I said in a deep movie-villain voice.

After the big lunch rush, Alexis got her break and came to meet us at the pool. We'd been able to secure lounge chairs after the lunch rush and had been laying in the sun, slathered in sunscreen. It was hot, and we were definitely ready for a dip. Alexis had on her swimsuit under her sundress, so she peeled off her outer layer and hurried in.

As Alexis swam the length of the pool underwater, Mia cried, "Oh no! She left her watch on!" But as Mia awkwardly tried to rush into the pool to grab Alexis, she slipped and kind of fell in.

"Mia!" gasped Katie.

We both jumped in, and as I went under, I heard a whistle blow, and then there was a huge splash.

When I popped up someone was pulling Mia to the side of the pool.

Mia was sputtering, and Katie and I gathered around, with Alexis swimming up alongside us.

"Mia! What happened? Are you okay?" Alexis said in alarm.

The person who had jumped in after us was a lifeguard—a young guy. He held Mia's arm and looked at her in grave concern. "Did you hit your head? Twist an ankle? What happened?"

Mia was fine now that she'd had a minute to breathe. She dunked under and smoothed her hair back off her face, then resurfaced, laughing in embarrassment.

"I saw that Alexis had gone in with her new watch on, but when I went to tell her, I slipped like a klutz and fell in. I'm okay, though."

"Darn!" said Alexis, looking at her watch and smacking the water in frustration. "Thanks, Mia." She jumped out and took her watch off to dry on a towel, and then she hopped back in.

"Sorry to cause a scene. I feel like such a spaz!" Mia laughed.

"Don't be sorry," the handsome young lifeguard said. "You're not a spaz. Accidents happen here every day." He smiled widely, revealing perfectly straight, white teeth that contrasted with his wavy jet-black hair and deeply tanned skin. "Hi. I'm Luis. I'm one of the new lifeguards around here."

"I'm Mia," Mia said, looking starstruck. "And these are my best friends, Alexis, Katie, and Emma."

"*You* I recognize from my lunch break," Luis said, pointing at Alexis, who grinned and waved. "Nice to meet you, other friends." Then he gently put a hand on Mia's arm. "Are you sure you're okay?"

"I'm fine, Luis," Mia said. "Thank you."

"Well, I work here from one o'clock to five o'clock every day during the summer," Luis said. "But I usually get here around noon, if you'd ever like a free swimming lesson." And he gave Mia a huge heart-melting smile.

"Oh, but Mia—" Alexis began, and I saw Mia kick her under the water.

"Can always use a few pointers," Mia finished for her. "I will remember that. Thanks, Luis!" she said. She smiled sweetly at him.

And with another dazzling grin, Luis was back to his post.

Once he was gone, Alexis gave Mia a look. "You're already a *great* swimmer, Mia," she said.

Mia smirked. "I know that and you know that,

but does Luis, the cutest lifeguard ever, need to know that? I don't think so."

"He *is* cute," I agreed, and Katie nodded with a huge smile.

Alexis sighed. "I don't like the sound of this," she said.

Mia fluttered her eyelashes at Alexis. "There's always room for improvement!"

"Hey, Alexis!" I said, thinking about how we planned to hopefully make Alexis's working situation better. "We had a pretty great idea at lunch. We are going to bake some cupcakes after this, so you can bring them in for Miss Mary Jane tomorrow to sweeten her up. What do you think?"

"Ha! It's going to take a lot more than cupcakes!" she said. "But thanks. If you could please make a bunch, I'd love to share them with Aldo, who does the cooking, and the kid, Finn, who's my helper. I'd even give one to Mrs. Chilson."

"Great," we agreed.

"And I'll personally deliver them myself tomorrow, just in time for my swimming lesson!" joked Mia.

"Oh brother," said Alexis. "I don't want any part of this!"

She left to change into her work clothes while

the rest of us played a loud game of Marco Polo with a bunch of kids from school.

The rest of the afternoon passed quickly, and though we left before Alexis had finished work, she promised to check in with us when she was home and showered.

We went back to Katie's to whip up a basic batch of vanilla cupcakes. We were going to make some with vanilla frosting and some with chocolate frosting, since we weren't sure if Mary Jane was a chocolate or vanilla person.

While we waited for the cupcakes to cool so we could frost them, Katie's mom telephoned from work, and Katie took the call in the next room. I didn't mean to eavesdrop, but I couldn't help overhearing everything from where I was sitting.

The modeling agency had followed up, and Katie had a test shoot booked for Monday with a local photographer I knew. I could hear the excitement in Katie's voice, and the feelings of annoyance rose in me again. I pushed them down and focused on what a great friend Katie is and how smart she is and that she's a talented chef. And I reminded myself that times change, and I might get a call for a great job soon. I took deep breaths and sampled both frostings, which were extra delicious.

Katie came bounding back from the other room, her eyes bright with excitement.

"Guess what? I have a test shoot on Monday!" she said excitedly.

"Cool beans!" crowed Mia.

"Nice," I said, trying to be a better person than I was.

Katie turned to me. "Oh, Emma! Is there any way you'd be willing to come with me? I'm so nervous, and I have no idea what to do! My mom can't go because she's booked solid at work, and Jeff is out of town next week at a teachers' conference. And there's no way my dad would go. Please?" Her big brown eyes looked so hopeless and scared, how could I say no?

I took a deep breath. "Sure," I said. "I'm free, and I'd be happy to go with you."

She threw her arms around me. "Thank you so much, Emma!"

I patted her on the back. "No problem."

I wondered if I'd ever model again, or was I just doomed to become Katie's manager for life? A has-been? All washed up as an early teen? I tried to think happy thoughts, but it wasn't easy.

Mia asked, "Will you girls be back in the city?

You could pick up some of those insanely delicious A Summer Day cupcakes!"

"Oh, the shoot is local, but I think I learned the cotton candy trick!" said Katie. "It's cotton candy extract! Can you believe there's such a thing? It's only three dollars a bottle, and Jeff promised he'd pick some up for me today on his way home."

"Great!" I said. "We can make them on Friday during our regular session."

"I'm still not sure how they got that frosting to taste like soft-serve ice cream," said Katie. "I've been googling, but nothing is coming up."

"We can tinker with ideas," said Mia. "I'm not worried. Even if we just end up doing vanilla with sprinkles in the end, I still think it will be delicious with the cotton candy cupcake."

We frosted and boxed the vanilla and chocolate cupcakes, and soon, it was time for my dad to pick me up. We all made a plan to meet the next day at the pool, a little later this time, and Katie would bring the goodies. (We didn't trust Mia to bring them. She might give them all to Luis!)

CHAPTER 5

Work, Work, Work!

The next day we met at the pool at one o'clock and cut the long lunch line to drop the cupcakes to Alexis. We did the same thing as we did yesterday: We saved ourselves a table, knowing the loungers would open up later, and we got in line to order lunch. Today I was going for a grilled cheese and French fries. There weren't lots of healthy options. I wondered if Alexis's mom made her pack her own lunch.

As the line snaked toward the front, we could see that there was an adult woman behind the counter with Alexis, hustling around to help get the orders ready. "Smiley" Mary Jane was nowhere to be seen.

Alexis looked happy, despite the frantic pace, and she and the woman seemed to work well together, joking as they moved around the small space in sync, helping each other out by grabbing things for each other and handing them over, like Cokes from the back cooler or a shake that was ready to be taken off the machine for someone else's order. There was music playing—not too loudly, but fun sounding—and Aldo was bopping around to it in the back while Finn hustled around with a smile on his freckled face.

Alexis seemed so mature to me as I watched her just then. It was almost like she was this woman's equal. She was breezy and efficient, and they seemed to be in flow, kind of calmly but busily getting the work done.

Since we were a little later today, there was no one in the line after us, and Alexis was able to catch her breath.

"Hey, Mrs. Chilson! These are my friends who made the cupcakes."

"Oooh, wonderful! Hi, girls! Let's all have one now while things are calm," she said.

Alexis grabbed the cupcake carrier, which was covered with Cupcake Club stickers that my brother Matt had designed for us, and she offered them around to everyone, including Finn and Aldo. Us Cupcakers declined, since we hadn't had lunch yet, but Alexis's three coworkers moaned and sighed as they each devoured a cupcake.

"Fantastico!" said Aldo, the fry master.

"These are insane," agreed the kid, Finn.

"Girls, you are so talented!" said Mrs. Chilson. "Wow!"

"Well, as you know, we do have a business doing it," said Alexis.

"Yes, that's right! I remember that from your résumé," said Mrs. Chilson. "Oh look! Here comes Mary Jane. Yoo-hoo! Mary Jane! Have one of Alexis's cupcakes that she brought as a treat for all of us!"

I wondered why Mrs. Chilson was fawning over Mary Jane so much. Wasn't Mrs. Chilson the boss and Mary Jane the employee?

Mary Jane stomped up to the window.

It was the moment of truth: Would she eat one of our best cupcakes and instantly be transformed from a pumpkin into a lovely princess?

But no. It wasn't to be.

"I'm gluten-free," scowled Mary Jane, poking away the cupcake Mrs. Chilson was offering her.

We all deflated. Our plan was foiled.

"And anyway, employees shouldn't be eating while they're on the job. It's in the bylaws, if you've read them," Mary Jane continued with a frown.

Mrs. Chilson winced and closed a napkin around her cupcake wrapper, balling it in her fist. "Yes, of course. You're right. Sorry, kids, I forgot. Back to work. No more eating on the job."

Mary Jane went back up behind the counter, and Mrs. Chilson came out to say good-bye to us. "Girls, I'm back to my desk for now. Great job on the cupcakes, and thank you so much for bringing them in for us. They were marvelous!"

I looked up at Alexis and saw that her smile had faded as she concentrated on cleaning up and restocking the area, with the help of a serious-looking Finn. Aldo was cooking furiously in the back, and Mary Jane had found a stool somewhere and sat herself on it like some sort of supervisor. The music was off, and people's heads were down as they went about their business. It was amazing how one teenage girl could bring down the mood of so many people at once.

Poor Alexis.

We began talking quietly among ourselves about unimportant things, and when our orders came up, we retreated to our table in a somber mood.

"What I don't get at all," began Mia, leaning in and speaking softly over her tuna melt, "is why

Mrs. Chilson even hired that girl? Was she helpful *before* Alexis came?"

"Yeah, 'cause she sure doesn't do anything now!" said Katie, stealing a glance back at the order window.

"And why is Mrs. Chilson so nice to her? Isn't Mrs. Chilson the boss?" I added.

We chewed and pondered one of life's many mysteries.

Just as we finished, we heard someone call out "Mia!"

It was Luis. Mia lit up when she saw him, and he came by the table to chat for a minute. After exchanging pleasantries he said, "I'd better get going. I just came to refill my water bottle. Aunt Janee's covering for me."

"Aunt Janee?" Mia said in confusion.

"Mrs. Chilson. She's my aunt," said Luis.

"Oh! She's so nice," said Mia.

"I know," added Luis. "That's how I got the job."

"Cool," said Mia.

"Yup. Lucky for me they're pretty big on nepotism around here," he said as he wandered off. Then he turned back. "Hey, don't forget! No swimming for an hour after you eat!"

I saluted him and Mia waved, and then he left.

"What on Earth is 'nepotism'?" I asked.

Katie's fingers flew over her phone screen as she searched for the definition of the word. "I was wondering the very same thing. Oh. Here it is. It's when people with power favor family members, mostly by giving them jobs or important positions. Huh."

"I wonder what he meant by that," said Mia.

I shrugged. "I don't know, but I *do* know that I'll soon be in an important position on a lounge chair, favoring some summer reading for the next hour!"

"Ha-ha," said Katie as we stood and gathered our things. We waved to Alexis, who gestured that she'd come swim with us soon, earning herself a dark look from Mary Jane, and then we were off.

Poor Mia was continuing her weird charade of not being a great swimmer, all so she could capture Luis's attention. It was ridiculous. Like, can you imagine faking that you were bad at something just so a boy who already likes you might like you more? It was too weird. When Alexis came into the pool during her break, she called to Mia to join us, but Mia waved her off.

Alexis swam underwater to join us and blew a stream of water into the air when she surfaced. "What's up with her?" she asked, jerking her thumb toward Mia.

"Keeping up the I-can't-swim act for Luis," I said, shrugging. "Her loss."

"Too bad," said Alexis, turning away from Mia. "Guess what? I had a great idea!"

"What?" we asked.

"The pool is celebrating its fifth-year anniversary with a party next weekend. I thought we should ask Mrs. Chilson if we could do a cupcake order for the event! Wouldn't that be great?"

I laughed. "Remember what happened when we made the cupcakes for the swim team that time?" The indoor pool had been so hot that the frosting had melted and slid off all the cupcakes, causing a mini emergency.

Alexis and Katie smiled at the memory. "Yeah, but we thought fast and saved the day!" said Katie.

"Just like we always do!" added Alexis. "So should we pitch it?"

"Hey, we could make those A Summer Day cupcakes!" said Katie.

I splashed the water with my hand. "Genius! We're doing the testing on Friday, so, Alexis, you can bring some samples over here on Saturday, okay?"

"It's a plan," agreed Alexis. "Now let's go hang out with Mia for a minute before I have to go back to work."

On Friday, the Cupcake Club got together for our usual baking session, and to bake a test batch of our version of A Summer Day cupcakes. Figuring out the right amount of cotton candy extract was the hardest part. Luckily, Katie had separated out our basic batter into four bowls and was testing different amounts of extract in each. She was so good at figuring out all the ratios and very organized in keeping track of which cupcakes were which. I was impressed, and it made me a little less mad about the modeling thing. I was lucky to have a friend like her, and it was cool how hard she was working on behalf of our business.

I was busy baking our weekly order of mini vanilla-frosted vanilla cupcakes for our client, Mona, who ran the bridal store. She gave me my first big break in modeling, and she was our first regular cupcake client. She had a standing weekly order of a few dozen mini cupcakes (the size of a quarter) that were in a nonstaining white color that matched her bridal shop.

"Grrrr!" Katie growled after tasting the third batch of cotton-candy cupcakes after they cooled. "I just can't get this right. It either tastes like cough syrup or like nothing!"

Mia had an idea. "What if I ride a bike over to the drugstore and buy some of that cotton candy in a tub? You could put real cotton candy in the batter and see what happens?"

It seemed like a lot of effort, but Katie was at her wit's end. "I hate to make you do it, but it's a great idea. I just don't know what else to do. If you go, I'll whip up some more batter, and it will be all ready when you get back. Thank you."

Mia went off, and with Katie quietly measuring and mixing and Alexis updating our ledger (she keeps track of all our profits and expenses), I felt a happy sense of calm accomplishment. My friends and I had been working together for so long. We knew our roles, and we got along very well when we were working (and most of the time when we weren't working). In contrast to Alexis's experience at the snack bar, I felt very lucky to be in such a great work environment.

When Katie was finished she sighed. "I also don't know what to do for the frosting," she said. "I've been tinkering with some ideas, but nothing tastes like what the Three Sisters made for their icing. I feel like I'm losing my mojo. I'm not good at this anymore." She put her head in her hands wearily and shook her head from side to side.

"Hey! Katie, don't say that!" I said, coming to stand beside her. I patted her back. "I think you're great at recipe development!"

Katie looked up and laughed darkly. "You should see the people at my dad's restaurant. *They're* great at it! I feel like my taste buds are all confused. Now I overanalyze everything, when before I only cared if things tasted good or bad. Now there are all these other things to consider, like acidity and balance and mouthfeel and finish. *Ugh!* I'm so confused!"

"Okay," I said patiently. "Take a deep breath. Don't overthink it. What if Alexis and I taste things for you for a little while and give you a break. Don't worry. Your skills will come back. You just have to get those other voices out of your head, you know?"

She sighed. "I guess."

Mia came in the back doorway then. "Ta-da!" She held a white plastic shopping bag aloft. "I wasn't sure how much to get, so I got three."

"Great," said Katie. "Let's try it." She set about pulling bunches of fluff from the tubs and packing them into measuring cups, muttering to herself and making notes on a legal pad. She'd add different amounts to the batter, and then she'd scoop the batter into the wrappers in the muffin tins and slide the tins into the oven.

When they were ready and slightly cooled, Katie laid them out in a row. "These have the most cotton candy, these have a medium amount, and these have the least," she said, pointing to each group of cupcakes in turn. "Let me know what you think." Then she folded her arms and leaned back against the counter while we got to work tasting.

I started with the medium-flavored ones, figuring it was our best bet. It was tasty but very sweet. I moved to the least sweet, and it seemed great, almost identical to the one from Three Sisters.

. Mia had started with the sweetest one and winced as she spit her bite into the trash. "Awful," she said, shaking her head. She gulped some water and joined me at the least-sweetened batch. After her first bite she nodded and jabbed her finger at them. "Mm-hm," she said, through a mouthful of crumbs. "It's this one."

Alexis stepped in and went right for the one we both liked. She chewed thoughtfully and then said, "This one, definitely, but maybe reduce the sugar in the batter by like a quarter." *Zingo!* We had our recipe!

Next Katie pulled three small bowls of frosting out of the fridge and handed around Popsicle sticks, which is what we use to taste our frostings. (Spoons are a hassle to clean, and fingers are unprofessional!)

We took a small dab of each icing and swirled them thoughtfully in our mouths. One was too milky. It was kind of runny and plain, so I vetoed it. The next one tasted like cream cheese frosting. It was okay but kind of salty. And the third was our usual buttercream. It actually tasted really good on the cupcakes, but it wasn't the same as A Summer Day.

We were stumped, and I shared Katie's frustration. Our memory of the perfect cupcake was so good, but it was so hard to recapture.

Finally, Alexis ventured an idea. "What if we did ice cream–covered cupcakes? Like made frosting from actual ice cream?"

"And nothing else in it? Just whipped ice cream?" asked Katie, staring at the floor while she thought about it.

"Uh-huh," said Alexis. "We'll use the walk-in fridge at work to store them until the party started."

"They'd have to be eaten pretty fast," said Mia.

"When have you ever seen our cupcakes eaten slowly?" joked Alexis. "Seriously!"

We laughed. "It's a good idea," said Katie. "I have some vanilla ice cream in the freezer. Let's try it now."

She quickly loaded a pint of vanilla into the stand mixer and let it blend while she readied her cake piping kit. When the ice cream was smooth but not runny, she loaded it into the cloth bag, attached the piping tip that she liked, and piped ice cream onto four cupcakes. She put the frosting bag down, and we counted down to our tasting.

"One, two, three," said Alexis, and we all took bites.

"Oh wow!" I said.

"This is it!" agreed Mia.

"Totally easy and doable!" Katie said and grinned. "Who'd have thought it would be so easy?"

"And it's so economical! Only two new ingredients: cotton candy and ice cream. Yum!" bragged Alexis.

"We've got ourselves a recipe, girls!" I said.

"Look out, Mary Jane!" cried Mia.

CHAPTER 6

Professionals

$\mathcal{A}$lexis reported back from the pool on Saturday by text.

> We're in! Mrs. C. loves them and wants ten dozen for next weekend's party! Yahoo! Gotta figure out pricing later!

I was psyched. I love it when we work hard on something, and then it turns out well. It feels so good. The same couldn't be said about the start of Katie's modeling career.

On Monday morning her mom dropped us off at the photographer's studio. She had spoken to him by phone about how the photos should look (wholesome and not too much makeup), and my mom had assured her that he was a good guy.

Katie was nervous, and I felt bad for her. I squeezed her hand as we waited to be buzzed in, and I tried not to act too confident. This was my turf, and I wasn't nervous at all. Once you get to a photographer's studio—except when you're doing head shots for your portfolio—you've already got a job, so there's no need to worry. Photographers want the models to look as good as possible—their jobs depend on them getting great shots.

Inside, we checked in at the reception desk, and the receptionist directed us to a changing room in the back. Katie put on her first look, which was dressy. The ad agency had wanted to see her dressy, casual, and sporty, so she'd brought outfits for each.

The first was a lacy beige dress that was very dressy. Poor Katie did not look comfortable in it—she kept sucking in her stomach and holding her shoulders up unnaturally high—but it was too late to say anything other than "You look nice!"

We stopped by the hair-and-makeup area. The staff applied some very light makeup and curled her hair to make it look a little neater and more uniform in its curls. I had to admit, Katie did look very pretty. It wasn't a traditional knockout look, but she appeared sweet and wholesome and would be perfect for certain kinds of ads, like milk or juice or sneakers.

They sent us to wait on a bench outside the studio, and we could hear heavy metal music booming out from behind the door. Katie widened her eyes and looked at me.

I laughed. "The model gets to pick the music, don't worry."

"Phew!" said Katie, relieved.

I patted her knee. "It's not brain surgery. You'll be fine."

"I hope so. Every cell in my body is screaming at me to get out of here."

"Well, just try it this once and see what you think."

I couldn't believe I was now *convincing* Katie to model. How the tables had turned! I guess I felt good about myself because I knew the drill here, and she was so nervous. It wasn't a nice feeling to think that her fear made me stronger and kinder, but it was the truth.

Suddenly, the door flung open, and an Amazon strode out—a six-foot-tall, gorgeous woman, with long streaming hair, tons of makeup and tattoos, and a ball gown on—with the loud music trailing out behind her. She was intimidating, actually almost scary-looking, and Katie cowered against me. But then the woman waved at us and smiled, and Katie relaxed again.

A girl with green spiky hair and a clipboard appeared. She looked at me. "Katie?"

I shook my head and pointed at Katie.

"*You're* Katie?" the girl said, not even trying to hide her surprise.

Katie gulped and nodded.

"Right this way," said Green Hair.

We entered a black-painted hallway and then walked along until we took a hard left into a huge darkened studio. The music had been turned down, and there were a number of people there, fiddling with cameras and lights, cleaning up props, rolling up huge drop cloths from the floor. A fan whirred noisily, keeping things cool, and a man up on a huge ladder cried, "Emma, *darling*!"

I waved. "Hey, Victor!"

He clambered down and came across the room to me, both arms outstretched. "Oh, Emma, you are lovelier than ever! Team, look at our little Emma blooming!" He kissed me on both cheeks and held me out again at arm's length, looking admiringly at me and beaming. I had to laugh.

"You look good too, Victor!" I said. He was wiry and short, with long gray hair, and dressed from head to toe in black.

"Ha!" he cried, waving his hand. "I am an old man. A has-been. Now who have we here today?"

Katie was so nervous she couldn't even smile. "I'm Katie Brown," she said meekly.

I wanted to boss her and say, "Stand up straight! Be confident! Don't worry!" But of course I couldn't embarrass her, so I didn't say anything.

"And we are doing what today?" Victor asked kindly.

"Um . . ." Katie looked at me.

I guessed I had to take over. "Well, Katie has booked a job and needs some test shots. She has a range of looks with her today, but she needs to keep it all wholesome, mainstream—you know. It's her first time doing this so any great shots could go into her portfolio for future use. The agency wants copies of the best shots."

Victor was nodding and sizing up Katie as I spoke. He gently lifted a piece of her hair and let it drop, and then he took out a light meter and held it next to her face. She winced and I giggled.

"He's not going to hurt you. Don't worry! He's just checking what he's going to need for lighting."

Katie gulped. "Okay."

Victor turned away from us and started calling out to his assistants to get Katie's shoot set up. She stood there stock-still and wide-eyed, just taking it all in.

"So he'll stand you over there, in front of that wall. The lights, and maybe the fan, will be on you. Sometimes an assistant stands close to you with one of those big round things that bounce the light around. Victor will try different cameras and flashes and filters, and sometimes he gets a little cranky when he can't get the shot the way he wants it. Don't take it personally. He's really good and really nice and very professional. Just do what he says, and you'll be fine."

Katie nodded. "Okay," she whispered.

After a few minutes of standing around (there was always a lot of standing around in modeling), Victor called Katie into position.

I wasn't sure if I should stay in the room or go. Modeling can be a little embarrassing. They make you do dorky things and smile in ways you would not normally. I didn't want to make Katie self-conscious by watching her, so when I caught her eye, I jerked my thumb toward the door and waved good-bye.

But panic showed on her face, and she shook her head emphatically, indicating that I should stay. So I shrugged and found a director's chair that was out of everyone's way, and I took a seat to watch.

One of the assistants asked Katie if she wanted to pick the music, and I was proud of Katie when she said yes. The only bummer was that she picked a folk music channel, and it brought the energy down a bit. When you have that many people in the room, it works better if you make it feel like a party, with great, loud music. It sounds silly, but I just know from experience how it works.

Victor started out as his usual charming self. He looked through the lens and began complimenting Katie. "Oh yes. I see why they picked you. Your skin is lovely. So fresh. Very natural. I love it!"

He started clicking, getting Katie warmed up, getting a feel for her best angles. This is usually the part when the model relaxes and begins to trust the photographer. With the best photographers, it only takes a minute or two, and Victor was one of the best.

Only it wasn't working.

After a few minutes Victor sighed. "Okay, Miss Katie. Pretend you're in your happiest place. Where is that?"

Katie thought for a minute. "The kitchen?" she said, and her eyes lit up.

"Yes! Good. I like this," said Victor. He began clicking enthusiastically, but it didn't last. He paused again and called to one of his assistants.

"Miranda, soften the hands for me. Shake out the shoulders."

The assistant scurried into the frame and made some adjustments, then stepped away, her head tilted to the side, considering Katie. Victor looked through his camera and sighed again.

"Maybe it is the outfit. Katie, let's start with something you feel comfortable in. Run back and change into something happy."

I wasn't sure if I should go with her or not, so I stayed put while Katie ran back to the changing room. She was back in a flash, in beat-up jeans and a loose, white button-down over a tank top.

Victor clapped his hands when he saw her. "Yes! Much better. This is the real Katie. Now we will get the shot."

He tried for a little bit, but even from where I was sitting, Katie looked stiff and nervous. Victor conferred in whispers with his assistant, and Katie started to look miserable. I felt so bad for her, but I was helpless. Unless . . .

"Victor!" I hopped up and crossed the room to his side.

"Emma, darling! A true professional!"

I winced, knowing this was kind of a dig against Katie. "What if I give Katie some distraction, off-frame? Something to react to?"

Victor shrugged. "Worth a try."

I walked over to Katie, who looked even more upset than before. She knew everyone was getting very frustrated with her and that we were all talking about her.

She clutched at my shirt. "Emma! This is so hard! I had no idea. I can't believe you do this all the time. It's . . . embarrassing!"

"Okay. Don't worry. It's like this for everyone the first few times. . . ."

"*Few* times?"

"Look. I'm going to talk to you from the side, and I'm going to tell you some stories to distract you. I want you to listen, but try to look at Victor as much as possible, okay?"

Katie nodded miserably.

I started with a story of some hijinks by my little brother, Jake, and Katie smiled a real smile.

Victor said, "Good, good," quietly, so as not to get Katie off track, and I kept going.

Next I told her some funny Alexis stories from when we were in preschool, and that got a giggle.

"Yes!" said Victor. "This is working!"

I got her actually laughing with a story about our sometimes-enemy Olivia Allen, but Victor stopped me. "No laughing! Too much! Some giggles are okay, but I only want smiles, not open mouths."

Katie seemed to remember where she was and got somber again, so I had to warm her up again.

It was tiring, but after a bit I could tell Victor had some shots he liked.

"Okay, final change!" said Victor.

Katie ran off to put on the skirt and top she'd brought, and Victor came to my side while his assistants fiddled with all the equipment.

"Emma, you saved us today!" he said. "That was not going well. Thank you so much!"

"No problem, Victor. I was the one who got her into this mess, so I felt like it was the least I could do. I don't want to see her fail."

And I realized it was true. As annoying as this whole thing was—with Katie getting the campaign I'd tried out for—she was still my friend, as my mom said. And jobs come and go, but great friends should be forever.

Katie popped back in, and I could see she was

more comfortable now. She knew Victor had had some success, and that had built up her confidence. This time I took a spot on her other side and got her smiling, talking about food and crazy recipe ideas.

After another fifteen minutes Victor came out from behind the camera.

"We've got it," he announced.

Katie came out of the shooting area, and we high-fived.

"Thank you, Victor. I'm sorry I was such a newbie. I had no idea how hard this was going to be," she said, offering her hand for him to shake.

He took her hand and clasped it warmly. "It was a pleasure, Katie. You can't imagine how many divas I work with. I'd choose a newbie over that drama any day."

Victor double-kissed me again. Katie and I thanked everyone and said our good-byes, then we retreated to the changing room. Inside, Katie flopped onto the canvas butterfly chair and sighed heavily.

"*That* is tiring work. I'd rather be on my feet in a kitchen all day than do that every day. I'm really impressed that you can make a job out of it."

I smiled. It was kind of nice for one of my

friends to have a sense of how hard I work when I model. I know I always say "It isn't brain surgery," but the truth is, it's a different kind of hard. It takes nerves and stamina and energy and a certain kind of charm. And considering that it's all about how you look, you can't afford to be self-conscious while you're doing it.

"Thanks," I said. "It takes practice. You learn to just flip the on switch when you go into a shoot, and you kind of do a mind meld with the photographer. That's why a lot of the time you see famous photographers favoring certain models. They find they work well together, and the pictures come out better than with other people."

Katie nodded. "Well, Victor and I aren't forming a partnership anytime soon, that's for sure!"

"You never know. That was only your first time. And you still have to do the coat shoot for the agency."

Katie sighed. "I just have to focus on the fact that it's a job and it's not about me."

I nodded. "It's funny, isn't it? It's kind of all about the model, but the model doesn't really matter in the end. She's just a stand-in for the viewer to imagine herself there."

"I think I'm better off in a kitchen. We'll see."

"You did great for your first time. Don't worry. The campaign will be fantastic, and people will love it!"

Little did I know how it all might soon end up backfiring one day.

CHAPTER 7

Showtime!

When I got home my mom said there was a message on the voice mail for me. It was Lindsay Miller, from the Three Sisters cupcake store!

"Hi, Emma! It's Lindsay Miller. It was great to meet you the other day. Thanks so much for e-mailing me your number. I'm just calling to follow up on the possibility of working with you for our campaign. Could you or your guardian please give me a call at the shop when you have a minute? Thanks so much! Bye!"

I smiled. It would be fun to work with Three Sisters, and it would be cool to do a national campaign. I didn't expect that they'd pay me much, but it would be great exposure and awesome for my portfolio. Plus, I'd get to have some more A

Summer Day cupcakes and maybe even find out the secret to their amazing vanilla ice cream–tasting frosting!

My mom promised to call Lindsay the next day to let me know the plan and give her my agent's contact information.

I texted Alexis to check in, but she was at work, so I did some summer reading and practiced my flute, which I hadn't touched in days. The afternoon flew by, and at five o'clock Alexis called. She was off work and wanted us all to go to the movies at the mall. I was up for it, so I arranged for my dad to drop us off. My brother Sam works at the movie theater at night, so he got us discount tickets, and soon we were all nestled into a romantic comedy with huge buckets of buttery popcorn.

When we came out of the dark theater after the movie, blinking in the bright lights of the mall, Mia clasped her hands to her chest and sighed. "That movie was so good! The boy was so sweet to the girl. I want a boyfriend just like him one day."

I rolled my eyes. Sometimes my friends were a little boy-crazy, and it bugged me.

"How about Luis?" joked Katie, glancing down at her phone.

"Oh, don't worry. I have a lesson booked with

him tomorrow!" Mia said with a big grin.

"Mia, you're a great swimmer! What on Earth are you thinking?" Alexis said indignantly.

"There's always room for improvement," said Mia, pouting.

"Hey! They booked the shoot!" Katie said gleefully, looking at her e-mail.

"I thought you already had a shoot," said Alexis.

"That was just a test. I go in on Friday to shoot the ad for the coats! Oh, thank you, Emma! Thank you so much for hooking me up and helping me out. You're the best!" She threw her arms around me for a huge hug.

I hugged her back. "You're welcome."

My annoyance with her had faded since Katie didn't seem all that interested in pursuing modeling anymore. Also, it felt good to help a friend who appreciated it. I figured I'd be okay with it as long as she didn't start showing up at all my gosees.

"My mom is going to come with me this time, so you're off the hook," said Katie.

"Okay, but just make sure she has some good jokes up her sleeve to get you to smile," I said, wagging a finger at Katie.

As we were deciding what to do next—get a

bite to eat or go home—who should walk by the movie theater but cranky Mary Jane Parks? Were we supposed to greet her? She didn't really know us and certainly hadn't made any effort to befriend us when we'd come to the snack bar. I looked at Alexis to follow her lead.

Alexis's eyes narrowed. Mary Jane was walking with two adults, both of them tall and blond, who seemed to be her parents.

"Wait a minute . . . ," said Alexis, just as Mary Jane drew near.

Mary Jane looked at Alexis and all of us, and then turned the other way and started a conversation with her parents, totally ignoring us.

"Hey!" said Alexis. "Hi, Mary Jane!" She said it in an almost angry voice, as if daring Mary Jane to ignore her.

Mary Jane turned and acted like she hadn't already noticed us. "Oh, hey," she said dismissively, like we were peasants and she was a queen. Her parents smiled at us, but the smiles weren't that friendly, and they all kept walking together.

"Wow!" said Alexis.

"What?" asked Mia. "Are you actually surprised she wasn't friendly?"

"No. That guy . . . Mary Jane's dad. I just put it

all together. I know him! He's the director of parks and recreation for our town!"

"Cool job," said Katie.

I shrugged. "So?"

"*So?* So he's Mrs. Chilson's boss!"

Realization dawned on us, and we turned and looked at one another in surprise.

"So Mrs. Chilson has to let Mary Jane work there, even though she's a totally useless, crabby girl!" crowed Mia.

At that we collapsed into giggles. Alexis laughed so hard she actually got tears in her eyes.

"Whoo! I feel so much better!" she said, drying her eyes. "I couldn't figure out what was wrong with me, and why—if I liked Mrs. Chilson and respected her so much—she seemed to favor Mary Jane. Now it all makes sense!"

"I wondered why she had Mary Jane working there in the first place. She never does anything but sit there and frown!" said Katie.

"And criticize me!" added Alexis.

"I can't believe it," I said. "Nepotism again!"

"Yes, but unlike Luis and Mrs. Chilson, it's bad nepotism." Mia shook her head. "That must've been what he was referring to when he mentioned there being a lot of nepotism around the pool."

"My mom always says anyone can help you get a job, but what you do with it is up to you." Alexis shook her head.

I thought of Katie in Victor's studio today. "True," I agreed. "Very true."

On Friday, while Katie was off at her coat shoot and Mia was having another lesson with Luis (since her dad had some business meetings and couldn't see her this weekend), I decided I'd head over to the pool and wait for Mia to be done so we could have lunch. We were meeting later at Katie's to bake for Mona and for the pool anniversary celebration the next day. I was excited to have some more cotton-candy cupcakes, that was for sure.

I was earlier than usual so I lucked out and found a lounge chair immediately. I spread my towel, laid out my summer reading book, and put on some sunscreen, then I went to let Alexis know I was there in case she wanted to take her break and swim with me. I spotted Mia heading into the pool with Luis, and I allowed myself a private little chuckle. Poor Luis. He had no idea he was teaching a girl to swim who was already a champion swimmer.

At the snack bar, Mary Jane sat on her usual

perch, frowning and criticizing Alexis. Alexis looked up in relief when I called out her name, and promised me she'd come meet me in ten minutes for a swim. I retreated to the pool and my book, but I couldn't even read—I was so distracted by Mia's act with Luis.

Luis was showing Mia how to breathe while swimming!

"I'm a little scared to put my head under," Mia said.

"Don't worry. I'm right here," Luis replied, patting her on the shoulder.

I couldn't believe my eyes. How long was Mia going to keep this up?

I watched for a few minutes more in stunned disbelief before Mia finally noticed me.

"Hi, Emma!" she shouted, and she waved from the water. "Be right there!" Then she turned and smiled at Luis. "Thanks so much, Luis," she said.

"My pleasure, Mia," Luis answered. "Anytime."

Mia hopped out of the pool and walked over to my lounge chair with a big grin on her face.

"I can't believe you did that," I said.

"Did what?" Mia said innocently. "Get a free swimming lesson?"

"A swimming lesson you don't need," I said.

"When are you going to tell him you swim like a pro?"

"Why does he need to know that?" Mia asked with a sly smile.

"Oh, Mia. This is not good!"

Alexis came over on her break and wanted to try the deep-diving pool. Unfortunately for Mia, she couldn't join us in the water because she couldn't let Luis know she knew how to swim. So she sat on the edge of the pool with her legs dangling in the water while Alexis and I had a blast seeing who could stay under the longest—the loser (Alexis) had to buy the winner (me) an ice cream. When Alexis exited the pool to return to work, she squeezed out her hair on Mia's shoulder, causing Mia to shriek and Luis to look over.

"Too bad you can't swim!" Alexis said loudly with an evil grin. "We missed ya!"

Mia looked over her shoulder to see if Luis had heard. "Shush!" she said to Alexis, and rolled her eyes. Then she winked.

"You're going to get caught!" I cautioned. "What will you do then?"

"Oh, please. It's harmless," said Mia. But she now looked unsure.

Our baking session that night was epic. Mrs. Brown had to go pick up pizzas for us because we didn't have a minute to make ourselves something to eat.

Every surface in the kitchen was covered with cooling cotton-candy cupcakes, and when Mrs. Brown came back from the pizza parlor, she laughed and said, "It smells like a carnival in here!"

She left the pizzas for us and retreated to her home office, away from the sugary smell.

Katie had been telling us about the shoot that day, which had been okay but not great.

"I just didn't feel or look like myself. It was like I was a blank canvas, and they decorated me however they wanted. It was weird," she said, pulling cooled cupcakes off a rack and setting them in a carrier. We'd be bringing them "naked" to the pool's party and frosting them on-site tomorrow.

"Welcome to modeling." I rolled my eyes.

"I have no idea how it's all going to turn out," she said. "My mom was trying to make me laugh, but it was a lot more formal than the other day, and the photographer wasn't as patient or nice as Victor," she told me. "He was a little scary, actually." Katie brushed some crumbs off her hands and began loading fresh cupcake liners into a tin for the next batch to bake.

"Bummer," I said. "Sometimes that happens. It's just bad chemistry, or he's under a lot of pressure or whatever."

"Yeah, well, depending on how the ad looks, I might not ever do it again. It's just not worth it to me. It's such a phony business, you know?" Katie closed the lid to the cupcake carrier and set it aside. She grabbed the final bowl of batter and a ladle and returned to the tin.

Yes, I did know. But now I was starting to get a little annoyed with Katie again. I mean, here she barges into my business uninvited, and now she's criticizing it?

"It's a living!" Alexis tried to lighten the mood with a joke, but she looked at me, and I could tell she knew I was getting irritated.

"Maybe for some people." Katie shuddered before ladling batter into the cupcake wrappers.

"People like our Emma!" Alexis said brightly, crossing the room to put an arm around my shoulder. Was she hugging me or holding me back from attacking Katie? It was hard to say. I took a deep breath in through my nose.

"It's not for everyone," I said through gritted teeth.

"And let's leave it at that," said Alexis.

Katie seemed to come out of her clueless daze as she finished her task. She looked up from the cupcake tin and said, "Oh. Sorry, Emma. I didn't mean you. I don't mean to be negative. I'm just bad at it, is all. Sorry."

She did look sorry, but at that moment I just wanted her to be quiet.

"Let's have pizza!" Mia said in a bossy and cheerful voice. "Now!"

Katie slid the last tray of cotton-candy cupcakes into the oven, and we all grabbed slices and sat down to eat.

The pizza took our minds off our troubles for a moment.

"The party's going to be fun tomorrow," said Alexis. "They're closing off the street and bringing in a carnival for the day!"

"Awesome!" I said.

"So we were right on theme with the cotton candy!" said Mia.

"Yes. And there's going to be a dunking booth," Alexis said wickedly. "I hope Mary Jane takes a turn in there!" She cackled and rubbed her hands together eagerly.

"I bet there'll be a huge line for that if she does," I said with a smile.

"Yes, but Finn, Aldo, and I get to cut it!" said Alexis.

"And Mrs. Chilson," added Katie.

"Right, but we won't even make her pitch the ball. She can just run up and hit the target with her bare hands to knock Mary Jane in," said Alexis, and we all laughed, imagining it.

"Our cupcakes will be a huge hit!" said Mia.

"For sure," agreed Alexis.

CHAPTER 8

Fallout

We were up early to transport the cupcakes to the town pool. The party was set to start at ten o'clock, and we needed to get some icing on at least a few dozen of the cupcakes to start.

Katie had whipped up a couple of tubs of the ice-cream frosting at home, and we kept them cold in my mom's huge, heavy-duty baseball team coolers in the back of our minivan. If the frosting got too soft, it would be a disaster.

"Beautiful day for a party," said my mom on the way to the pool. Then she asked casually, "Did anyone check the high temperature for the day?"

"Oh no! I forgot. Checking now!" said Alexis. "Oh."

"What?" Her "oh" had not sounded good.

"High of eighty-five degrees. Hmm."

We were all quiet for a minute while we pictured ice-cream frosting in eighty-five degree heat.

"Well, let's hope they'll go quickly!" said Mia.

"There's nothing we can do about it now," said Katie, looking out the window as we pulled up.

The carnival company was setting up, and people were milling around the street, getting ready. We saw Mrs. Chilson with a clipboard, and Alexis dashed over to double-check if it was okay to frost our cupcakes in the snack bar and leave them in the walk-in freezer until later. She agreed, and we began hauling the carriers and ice-cream tubs inside.

An SUV pulled up next to us, and I saw Mary Jane get out. She started hoisting bakery boxes from the new gluten-free bakery in the next town over, and her dad was helping her.

Huh.

When I caught Alexis's eye, I gestured to Mary Jane and her little project, and Alexis's eyes widened and then narrowed.

"She was talking about that the other day, saying it was unfair how gluten-free people are always penalized at events because there's nothing for them to eat."

Mia nodded. "It's true. My cousin is gluten-free, and she has to bring her own meals and snacks everywhere we go, just in case."

"Yeah, but Mary Jane could have asked us to bring a gluten-free alternative," said Alexis.

"Whatever. It's not like we're selling our cupcakes. People can just take what they want."

But as we passed by her SUV to unload the minivan, we realized that Mary Jane was doing just that: She'd set up a table right next to the carnival company's snack caravan, and she hung a sign that said GLUTEN-FREE HONEY CUPCAKES. $5 EACH.

"Five dollars each!" said Alexis, her eyes blazing. "Can you imagine? Who's going to pay that?"

Not too many people, as it turned out.

A little before the party got started, we found a nice shady spot on the street and set up the folding table that Mrs. Chilson had provided for us. Katie stayed in the snack bar, frosting a dozen or so cupcakes at a time and ferrying them out via a runner, who was either me or Mia. Alexis had to work during the morning shift, so we kept her updated on how the cupcakes were moving.

Mary Jane seemed to have few takers. We tried to ignore her, but she kept staring daggers at us. At one point she left her table, but then she came back

92

again with Mrs. Chilson, pointing at us and gesturing toward her table and ours.

Mrs. Chilson came over with an embarrassed look on her face. "Girls, I'm glad it's going so well. Unfortunately, Mary Jane is overheating in the sun, and her cupcakes are melting. We were wondering if you might be willing to trade the shade for a while this afternoon?"

"Um, I think it might be tough because we're giving away ice cream–frosted cupcakes," I said. I didn't want to be rude, but we could not sit in the sun with these things.

"I figured as much," said Mrs. Chilson. "Okay. Let's see what I can do to make some room in the shade for Mary Jane."

"We could share our table with her?" Mia suggested as Mrs. Chilson walked away.

Mrs. Chilson turned back and grinned. "Great idea. Thanks, girls."

But it was not to be. After a brief, heated discussion with Mary Jane at her table, Mrs. Chilson disappeared, and then the next thing I knew, Mary Jane's dad, who we'd seen in the mall, was at our table.

"Kids, I'm so sorry to be the bearer of bad news," he began. He didn't seem sorry as he was saying it, though. "Mrs. Chilson and I have had a miscommunication, and the town can't authorize the distribution of baked goods from a kitchen that hasn't been certified by the health department. I'm sorry to let you know you're going to have to take the cupcakes away now."

"What?" My face felt hot, and I was shocked. We'd never encountered anything like this before.

"But we cater lots of functions. We've never had a problem . . . ," said Mia.

Mr. Parks looked fake-regretfully at us. "Well, when you're dealing with the government, you know. . . ." He shrugged. "Thanks for understanding." And he walked away.

Mary Jane seemed to be intentionally looking away from us, but I knew she had to be behind all this. She was acting way too casual.

"What now?" asked Mia.

I took a deep breath. "Let's set up right outside the carnival limits," I suggested.

Mia looked at me and grinned. "Genius!"

And while we certainly got a lot more attention once we were right outside the entrance, we were also now in the bright sun, and it just wasn't working. The frosting was starting to slide off the cupcakes and form a puddle on the platter.

"Mia, we need a Plan B," I said finally.

Mia ran off to consult with Katie and Alexis at the snack bar, and she returned with a grin. "Alexis's mom is coming, and she's bringing spoons and ice-cream cups. We'll just say we're giving away ice cream–covered cupcakes!"

Within half an hour we had our new setup, and it was even more popular than before. We were calling our cupcakes "Cupcake Cups" or "Cupcakes à la Mode" ("*à la mode*" means "ice cream on top" in French), and since it was after lunchtime, people were eager to have them.

On one of my trips back to the kitchen, I took a peek at Mary Jane, who was now in our prime shady position. She'd hardly made a dent in her cupcake supply, and I couldn't say I was sorry.

When we'd given away all our cupcakes, which had won rave reviews, Alexis had finished her shift and Mary Jane was on duty at the snack bar. We watched as Mary Jane and her dad transferred all her honey cupcakes to the snack bar, and she continued to try to sell them while we Cupcakers dove gratefully into the pool.

It had been so hot, and we were so desperate to cool off, that I think Mia forgot about her little act with Luis. She went straight into the diving pool in a perfect swan dive, and swam across it underwater.

Luis landed nearly on top of her when he dove in to save her again, and she came up sputtering.

"Luis!" said Mia, treading water.

He was trying to pull her to the side to safety.

"Luis, I'm fine! I can swim!" Mia said finally.

"What?" Luis stopped in the middle of the diving pool, also treading water now. He stared at Mia. "What do you mean?"

Mia was mortified. "I mean . . . I'm so sorry. I can swim. I always could. I just . . ."

Luis stared at Mia, openmouthed. Then he said, "You mean you were faking?"

Mia shrugged. "Kind of?" she said, palms up.

"Wow," said Luis. "That makes me a total idiot." And he swam away.

"No!" Mia called after him. But it was too late. With three brothers in my house, I knew what boys are like when they've been badly embarrassed. They need to go off and cool down for a while, and there's no talking to them about it ever again.

"Ugh," said Mia. The rest of us treaded water, staring at her. There was nothing to say. We'd all seen this coming, and we'd warned her. "I'm the idiot," she said quietly. Then she swam to the side of the pool and got out.

We looked at one another, unsure what to do.

Then finally, Alexis said, "No. Mary Jane's the idiot." And that broke the tension. We all laughed and felt a little better.

I was exhausted when I got home that night. It was still so hot that my dad turned on our central air-conditioning, which he usually refuses to do until August. I lay on my bed and listened to a flute piece I was trying to learn and just tried to cool off.

Suddenly, my phone rang, and I looked at the caller ID. Alexis.

"Hey!" I said wearily.

"Mrs. Chilson wants to carry our cotton-candy cupcakes in the snack bar for the rest of the summer!"

"Great!" I said. "But wait, how are we going to do the frosting?"

"Oh, she said just use regular vanilla frosting," said Alexis.

"Good. I was worried she'd hate us for maybe getting her in trouble with her boss and then that whole weird switching tables thing. So what about the health certificate?"

"Get this: She said he made it up! There's no such rule! They buy baked goods from lots of places, including her sister, who's an amateur muffin maker."

"Wow. That is so shady of him."

"Anyway, we came out of all that looking good. Mrs. Chilson said we were very flexible and easy to work with and always upbeat."

"Awesome!" I said.

"Uh-huh. And guess what else?"

"What?"

"I got Luis's number for Mia, and she texted him to apologize, and he texted her back, and now they're on this long chat."

"No way!"

"Yup. And one more thing . . ."

"Boy, you're just full of news tonight, aren't you, missy?"

"Yes. Mary Jane Parks got stung by a bee. You're welcome!"

I laughed, but more from surprise than that I was glad. "What?"

"I think it was because of the honey cupcakes. It was payback from the bees."

"Is she okay?"

"Of course she's fine. The bee died, though. I think it might have gotten a taste of Mary Jane's crabbiness."

"Oh, Alexis!" Now I was laughing for real. "You are too much!"

We hung up, and I spent a few happy moments calculating the bump in our weekly income that we'd get from adding another regular (seasonal) customer. Even if this was a hard-working summer, at least I was with my besties, and we were making money and keeping our good reputation.

CHAPTER 9

Now We're Cooking!

$\mathcal{M}$ia texted me on Sunday.

What's up for the week?

I have to go into the city again for that Three Sisters cupcake shoot, I texted.

Ooh, I'm dying to go to the city! Mia wrote back. And I want to get some more of their yummy cupcakes! May I join you?

I sat and thought for a bit. The last time I invited a friend into the city when I was modeling, it did not turn out well for me. But maybe I could convince my mom to bring the Cupcake Club, and they could shop or walk around while I did my shoot, and then we could meet up.

I checked with Mom, and she agreed, saying it was up to me, so I sent out a group text.

I have to go to the city for the Three Sisters cupcake shoot on Tuesday. My mom said you could all come. Anyone else in?

Katie was free and Alexis had the day off. So with Mia, they made a plan to go to some big cooking store and a museum while I had my shoot. We'd all meet up for lunch and then stop by the Three Sisters store afterward.

The morning of the shoot, Mom and I picked everyone up early, and when Katie got into the car, she said, "I have exciting news! Guess what? They've already posted some of my coat modeling pics on the store website as a fall preview!"

"No way!" said Mia, stabbing her phone with her fingers in excitement. Soon, she had it up on her screen.

"Wow, Katie! You look awesome!"

Alexis leaned in. "So pretty! Good job, Katie!"

I half wanted to see and half didn't. What if it was great, and then I felt awful? What if it was awful, and then I felt awful? It was a lose–lose situation. But I couldn't not ask to see.

"My turn!" I said fake-cheerfully.

Mia passed her phone to me in the front seat, and I took a deep breath. Looking down at the pictures I felt immediate relief. They were fine. Not amazing, not horrible, just fine.

"Wow, Katie!" I said, kind of hamming it up. "This is *great*!"

She smiled shyly. "Thanks. It's pretty cool."

I felt the old flare of annoyance, but I kept it hidden. I wanted to scream, *Oh, so now it's cool? What about when you were knocking modeling the other night and calling it a phony profession?* But I held my tongue.

"Can I post it?" asked Mia.

"Sure!" Katie said proudly. "I just put it up on mine and said 'Thanks for the opportunity.' But if you guys want to post it too. . . ."

I got the hint. "Oh, right. I'll do it now," and I quickly posted the link with the hashtag "#soproud."

Mean person that I am, I was half hoping she'd get a lukewarm response. I couldn't deal with her getting all into the modeling idea again, and I didn't want her to get too encouraged.

When we got to the city, they dropped me off, and my mom continued on to find parking while the other girls headed off on their adventure. I made my way upstairs in the loft building to what turned out to be a test kitchen and TV studio for cooking shows. Despite myself I half wished Katie had come to the actual shoot. This would be her idea of nirvana.

There was every cooking instrument you could imagine, and all sorts of baking accessories and machines. There were big bowls of cupcake batter and frosting and toppings that had been premade for the shoot. It looked like a Cupcake Club baking session but on a much higher level.

"Hey!" Lindsay Miller was there, and she introduced me to her sisters, Marnie and Isabelle. They were as nice as she was and very enthusiastic about the shoot.

The stylist took me in the back to try some different looks, and at some point my mom came up and settled in with a book. As I've said before, she isn't a huge fan of the modeling business, but she is a huge fan of women earning money. She sees all this as a good head start to my work future.

The stylist had me in a pale pink linen button-down, small gold hoop earrings, and white jeans. It was a very fresh look and shared a palette with the Three Sisters stores and logo. The sisters loved what I had on and added a pink-and-white–striped apron with THREE SISTERS on it to complete the look. Then I went in for hair and makeup.

They kept my look natural, and getting ready all went pretty fast. Soon, it was time for the shoot.

Much to my surprise, Victor and his team walked in.

"Emma! How lucky am I?" he cried from across the room.

The ad people and the studio staff turned and smiled at us as we embraced.

"Hey, Victor! I'm so happy it's you today. I had no idea!"

"Darling, thank goodness it's not that ghastly amateur again. What was her name? Kathy?"

I swallowed hard. I didn't want to publicly trash one of my best friends. "Katie. It was her first time. We all have to start somewhere," I said brightly. I had to change the subject. "And Katie's a good friend. I'm just happy you and I get to work together today!"

"Me too, doll." He linked his arm through mine and brought me over to the kitchen counter for some lighting checks.

Soon, we were on a roll, with Victor snapping away and the Three Sisters people all looking pleased. Victor kept up a steady stream of compliments:

"Love it, Emma! Perfect! Hold that! Yes!" I couldn't help but think what a contrast this was to the hard time Katie had had the other day.

There is something to modeling that is a little like acting. You definitely have to find some kind of inspiration for the happy faces and the open looks they wanted from you. You have to give yourself over to it completely.

We had a break while the ad people and Victor and the sisters reviewed what we'd gotten so far. They had me change my outfit and do another round of shots, and they were even happier with those. I started checking my watch after that, wondering when we might be finished. My friends and I were due to meet nearby at twelve forty-five, and it was already twelve fifteen. I still had to change, get off all the makeup, and walk the few blocks to where they were. I sat in a director's chair while the team chatted, deciding what to shoot next.

"Emma, darling!" Victor called. "We've got a problem with the files from the first outfit. We're going to need to get you back into that and reshoot a few of the poses."

Oh no!

I looked down at my watch again. I'd be late to meet my friends for sure. Maybe an hour or more!

Ugh, this whole idea was a bad one from the beginning. How many more times did I need to make the mistake of mixing business with pleasure before I learned my lesson?

But I'm a professional, so I smiled a huge smile and said, "Great. Be right back!"

Inside the changing room, I whipped off the clothes, being careful not to get makeup on them, and I quickly typed off a text to my friends, saying I was trapped for another hour.

While I tied the laces on the white sneakers I had to wear, I awaited a confirmation that they'd gotten my text.

Seconds later Mia replied, Can we come watch? We're all done here!

I paused. It might be kind of cool to have them see me. Then maybe Katie could get an idea of what went into it. I could scare her off a bit, so she wouldn't keep trying to copy me by being a model. Plus, they would think this place was really cool.

"Let me check," I said.

Minutes later, having received permission from everyone, I sent them the address.

See you soon, typed Mia.

❧

I looked over when my friends trudged in, but Victor said, "Emma! Yoo-hoo! Over here, please!" so I couldn't look again. I could see out of my peripheral vision that they were standing with my mom, though.

Victor was really hamming it up as he shot this round. I sometimes think photographers do all that just to keep themselves interested. He kept up his running commentary of "Yes, darling, beautiful, fabulous. Look over your shoulder. Softer hands. Perfect! Tuck the chin. Just right. Mmm-hmm. Turn your left shoulder a bit left and tip forward. You're brilliant!"

At this point I can follow these commands in my sleep, but if I were just starting out, I knew I'd find it superconfusing. Victor and I got into a mind meld for a while, and I could tell the shots he was getting were pure gold. He kept me moving around the set, though, and kept it going, tweaking the lighting to make me "glow" more and asking for all sorts of poses.

It was when we were almost done that I heard "Oh no!"

Victor stopped shooting and turned around, the mood broken.

The ad agency person had clapped her hand over her mouth. "Sorry! I didn't mean to interrupt," she said.

"Is everything okay?" Victor asked coldly. He was annoyed at having his concentration broken, I could tell.

The ad person had no choice but to explain. "We had a group of young baking sisters scheduled to come in for a shoot this afternoon. It was supposed to be like a tribute to these baking sisters. Only they had to cancel because one of them has appendicitis, and their mom couldn't drive the others in."

Everyone looked around at one another, unsure of what to do or say.

Then I took a deep breath. "My friends and I could do it," I offered. Then I looked at them. Mia looked psyched, Alexis looked surprised, and Katie looked mortified. "They're right over there. They'd love to be in it!" I lied, pointing. "And we have a business back home, baking cupcakes for events and parties. So we know our way around a kitchen." At least that part wasn't a lie.

Everyone turned to look at them, and when Victor spotted Katie, he turned to his assistant Green Hair and said something in her ear, and she snickered and rolled her eyes. Right then I hated them both, especially the assistant. Luckily, Katie hadn't seen them.

"What do you say, kids? Would you like to jump into costume and hop onstage? With your guardians' consents, of course," asked the ad agency lady. "No pressure."

They checked quietly with one another, and then Alexis spoke for them all. "Sure. We'll help out," she said.

"On one condition! The sisters have to tell us how to make their vanilla ice cream–flavored frosting!" joked Katie.

"Never!" cried Lindsay, also joking.

The girls were whisked away to the changing rooms, and everyone relaxed for a few minutes while we waited for them.

I went to check in with my mom, who was e-mailing permission forms to the other parents. There was a small buffet table next to her, and I grabbed half a sandwich, just to nibble on since my energy was starting to flag.

She looked up. "Are you okay with this?" she asked quietly.

I inhaled deeply. "Yes, I am. It's different when it has to do with cupcakes. Also when it's all of us together. It's not the same as me going head-to-head against a friend for a job."

She looked at me for an extra long time, trying to decide if I was being honest.

"I swear, Mom. I wouldn't have suggested it otherwise. For real," I said.

"Okay," she said, but it was in a tone of voice that implied she didn't totally believe me.

I paused, thinking about it for a minute. It had been a little impulsive of me make that offer. Maybe I needed to start being more protective of myself and my activities. Why did I always want to share with friends? I didn't know.

But the flip side was, it was always more fun with friends around, and I did enjoy when my two worlds collided for a little bit. Friends and modeling aren't a natural combination, but when you added cupcakes to it, it made it all right.

I stayed away from Victor and Green Hair during the break. I didn't want to let any of their anti-Katie negativity into my head. Luckily, this afternoon shoot was meant to be done with amateurs anyway, so having the Cupcakers there wasn't that much of a strain.

The ad lady came in and gave us all an overview of what they were looking for. Then Lindsay and her sisters came into the kitchen setup and gave us instructions on what to make and how to do it. And finally, Victor and his assistants used masking tape to block out our "marks," which tell us where we needed to stand and which way we needed to face to get the full shots they wanted.

Katie could not get over the test kitchen and its supplies. If we had one problem, it was that she was a little distracted by all the goodies it held and what she could do with them. Alexis was a ham, but it worked. She was joking around and making funny faces, but it got everyone laughing, including the adults, and created a relaxed atmosphere. Mia was the most nervous at first. She kept smiling a tight, awkward smile, and this time it was she who caused Victor's frustration. But she eventually settled down and lost herself in the decorating process when they handed her some baked cupcakes to decorate and a whole palette of toppings and decorations to use.

We worked for about an hour, all of us in pink and white, with striped aprons. Like always, we got into a rhythm as we worked together and lost track of time, and ourselves. We became the well-oiled machine that is the Cupcake Club.

By the end Victor was calling out compliments

to us, even Katie, and when he said, "That's a wrap!" all the adults burst into applause.

For us it was like waking from a dream. We were a little dazed and distracted, but it had been really fun, and we had a great pile of beautiful cupcakes at the end of it, which Lindsay offered around for everyone to eat.

Alexis pulled aside Marnie, the sister who seemed to handle the day-to-day of Three Sisters, and basically interviewed her about the cupcake business and their margins.

Katie grabbed Lindsay and asked all about recipe development. I could see their heads bent together as Lindsay made notes on a legal pad, and Katie copied them into her phone.

Mia and Victor hit it off, and they were chatting away, laughing their heads off.

I snuck away into the changing room and used baby wipes to take off the makeup. I put on my plain old jeans, my simple T-shirt, and my own sneakers, and then I just sat for a moment, relaxing. It had gone well. Thank goodness!

When I went back outside, the ad lady was hugging me, saying how grateful she was for my help and how I'd saved the day. She promised to up my rate and include a "finder's fee" for getting my friends into the act. The Miller sisters hugged me too, saying I had been a perfect choice, and it was fate that I'd come into their store that day while Lindsay was there.

My friends piled out of the changing room, still fully made-up but enjoying the novelty of their looks, and we all hopped into the huge freight elevator with my mom to head out.

"Bye, darlings!" Victor called as we left. I blew him a kiss. I needed him as a friend, professionally speaking, even if I didn't always agree with his behavior.

Once we left the building, Katie was all aflutter: She'd gotten the vanilla ice cream–flavored frosting recipe and learned the key ingredient was cornstarch!

Alexis was thrilled: Marnie Miller had asked her to stay in touch, saying they could use an intern in their office and maybe Alexis could come in and see how it all runs.

Mia was ecstatic: Victor had given her his card and was interested in shooting some of her fashions for her portfolio for free!

"Emma, you're the best friend ever! Thank you for making all this happen!" cried Mia, throwing her arms around me.

"Thanks, Em. You rock," said Alexis.

"Where would I be without you?" said Katie. "I mean it!"

I glanced at my mom, who was smiling proudly at me. She winked. "Time for some lunch, then cupcakes, right?"

"It's always time for cupcakes!" I said.

CHAPTER 10

Catwalks and Cupcakes

It was on the car ride back that we first noticed the fallout.

Alexis reached up to the front seat and wordlessly handed me her phone. I glanced down at it, and my eyes widened. It was a stream of comments posted on the link she'd put up about Katie's modeling.

They all said the same thing: "This girl's not a model. Come on! If she can do this, anyone can!"

And worse, much worse: picking apart her looks and her figure and her poses—everything.

My mouth went dry, and my stomach clenched. I looked at Alexis, frowning worriedly. Then I glanced at Katie, who'd fallen asleep against the car door, her head resting on the window.

"What do we do?" I whispered.

"Take down the links," said Alexis.

Quickly, I logged into my accounts and removed my posts. The comments disappeared with them. Alexis conveyed everything to Mia, who looked aghast, and did the same. There was only one problem. Katie's phone was in her hand, and we didn't know her password anyway.

How were we ever going to prevent her from seeing all that meanness?

We stared nervously at one another and at Katie's phone. Finally, Alexis reached over and tried to slide it out of Katie's grasp, but Katie woke right up. Mia gave a little gasp. She couldn't help herself.

"Hmm?" she said. "Are we home?" She wiped her eyes and looked out the window. Then she looked at all of us staring at her. We must've had awful expressions on our faces. "What?" she asked. "Was I drooling? Snoring?"

I took a deep breath. I owed it to her to deliver the news. "Katie . . . You remember how we talked about modeling being kind of a ruthless profession? And how you can't please all the people all the time?"

"Yeah?" she said, confused.

"Well . . ."

"Not everyone loves your ad campaign," said

Alexis, basically ripping off the proverbial Band-Aid. "Sorry. I couldn't drag it out," she said to me. Then she turned to Katie. "If I were you, I'd take down your post right now. Don't read any of the comments. Just take it down and move on."

"Girls?" said my mom, who tries to stay out of our conversations in the car. (She says she tries to be invisible because that's when she gets all the info we wouldn't normally tell her. Annoyingly, it kind of works.) "Everything okay?"

"Um . . . ," I said.

But Katie was already reading the comments, her face going pale.

"'Unprofessional,'" she whispered so quietly we could barely hear her. "'Ugly'? 'Fat'? 'Tacky'?" She covered her mouth with her hand. "Oh no!" Her eyes welled with tears, which quickly spilled down her cheeks.

"Um, Mom?" I said.

"Pulling over," said my mom, checking her mirrors and putting on her blinker. Then she said sharply, "Take the phone away."

Alexis grabbed the phone from Katie, and Katie let her, bringing her hands up to bury her face while she sobbed quietly. We were silent. We didn't know what to say or do. My mom parked in the

117

breakdown lane of the highway, then climbed out and flung open the door to the backseat, all very fast, like she used to when my little brother, Jake, would feel carsick. She took Katie in her arms, tight, and rocked her and patted her head and rubbed her back while Katie cried.

My mom stared grimly at the rest of us while we exchanged scared looks with one another. After a few minutes, Katie's sobbing subsided, and my mom pulled out a pack of tissues from her purse and gave it to her. Katie's face was a mess of running makeup from the photo shoot. I felt awful for her. She hiccupped.

"Why are people so mean?" she asked sadly.

"They're jealous," said my mom. "Plain and simple. And it makes them feel powerful to criticize others."

I thought of Victor and his snarky comments earlier about Katie. I could see that what my mom said was true. Some people build themselves up by knocking down others, but it's a bad way to be. I winced, thinking of how mean I'd been to Katie about her bedhead and everything on the day she got the job over me. It had made me feel better to knock her down, and that was terrible of me.

"I'm so sorry, Katie," I said.

She blew her nose and sighed. "I shouldn't have read the comments. You were right. I'll never unsee them."

"What kind of losers take the time to comment like that?" asked Mia.

"There are all kinds of people on the Internet who like hiding behind their computers and saying mean things about people. They're called trolls. It's a big problem. The thing is, and I know this sounds like a cliché, but you can't take it personally," said my mom. "They're just looking for someone to knock down for the slightest reason. It could have been anyone. It could be me tomorrow!"

"Or me!" I added.

Katie shook her head. "I hope not."

My mom took a deep breath. "Let's get you home now, okay? You need to see your mom and talk it out with her."

Katie nodded. The idea of seeing her mom brought fresh tears to her eyes.

"Katie, you're a beautiful girl. Don't take any of those comments to heart. Promise me?" Mom said.

"I'll try," agreed Katie.

I bit my lip as I looked at her. It hadn't happened to me yet (not counting the one time a wedding dress designer was mean to me because I had a broken nose at a fashion shoot), but sooner or later it would. This was where it helped to be a professional. I'd built up lots of good feedback so far in my career, so if I get some negativity, I can just focus on the positives. Also, I can see myself playing a role in the shoots, so it's not really me who's in the ad, if that makes sense. It's my character, Emma the Model.

I would explain all this to Katie later, but right now she needed only one thing.

I opened the Three Sisters cupcake box on my lap and offered her A Summer Day cupcake and a Sleepover Party cupcake. She took the Sleepover Party one with a little laugh.

"Thanks. Just what I needed," she said as she took a bite.

We dropped off all the girls, and when we got home, my mom called all the moms to let them know what had happened. She felt that everyone needed a talk with their mothers that night, and all the other moms agreed.

When I checked in with the Cupcakers the next morning, we compared notes and learned that all our moms had said the same thing. What they'd said was basically this: You can't worry about what other people say about you, especially about your looks. If you're doing the best you can and being kind to everyone, no one has the right to criticize you. They also said we needed to live our lives for ourselves and not for some imagined public who might or might not be watching at any time.

Alexis had work, and we planned to meet at the pool around lunchtime. She'd take her break with us, and we could all catch up.

But when we got to the pool, Alexis was on duty with Mrs. Chilson, and it was pretty slow, so she clocked out for her break right then. Her eyes were blazing with news as she jogged over to join us. She looked like she was going to burst from excitement.

"Guess what, people?" she called.

"What?" I replied, sure she was about to tell us anyway.

She sat down at the lunch table next to us and paused for dramatic effect. "Mary Jane quit!"

"No way!" cried Mia.

Alexis nodded, a huge grin on her face. "She told Mrs. Chilson that the working conditions were awful and that they worked her too hard. So she quit."

"But she never did anything!" Mia pointed out.

"I know. The whole thing's a joke."

"You don't think she'll cook up some way to get you or Mrs. Chilson fired, do you?" Katie asked nervously.

"Nah," said Alexis, waving her hand in the air. "Mrs. C. loves me. She just asked me to be the temporary manager until she can find someone older to run the snack bar. She said she'd give me the job if I were older, because I am totally capable of running it, but it wouldn't look so good for her to have a young teen in charge. I get it." Alexis shrugged. She had to know she would never lack for job offers in life.

"Wow. Your summer just got about a thousand percent better," I said.

"I know," Alexis said happily. "But I just came to tell you I don't really have time to swim with you guys today. I need to eat a quick sandwich, then I've got to help Finn restock the cooler, and I need to do some inventory so we can get an order into the wholesaler before the weekend rush. . . ."

"Oh boy. Watch out for the new temporary manager!" I said.

"The boss is in town!" joked Mia.

Alexis left us, and we waited for our food.

"So how's it going today?" I asked Katie gently.

She sighed. "Not great. I'm still pretty upset."

"I'm so sorry," I said, squeezing her hand.

"Your mom was so nice," she said.

I nodded.

"All our moms are nice," said Mia as she placed our food orders down in front of us.

"It's true. That's probably why we're friends. We were raised by nice people to be nice people!" I kidded.

"That, and we all love cupcakes!"

"And lifeguards," whispered Mia.

"Hey, girls!" said Luis, coming up behind us.

We greeted him and discussed the Mary Jane drama, speculating on her revenge.

"Oh, she's pretty harmless," said Luis. "She's always quitting stuff in protest, but she never follows up on it. She just enjoys being a bully."

"And you'd know all this from . . . ?" asked Mia.

"Oh, family reunions," said Luis, waving his hand dismissively. "Okay. Gotta get back to work now. See you gals at the pool later!" And he left.

We collapsed into giggles. "So Luis and Mary Jane are related, too? This nepotism thing is no joke!" said Katie.

"Listen, Katie," I said. "I don't want to keep

bringing it up, but maybe what you need is a good modeling experience. Something to cleanse your palate, so to speak? A fresh start?"

Katie waved her hands. "That's what you gave me yesterday. Thank you so much. It was fun to work with Victor again, and to be with all you guys and those nice Miller sisters. Plus, that kitchen space was amazing! The whole afternoon was great. I'm just focusing on that and blotting out the whole other thing. Sooner or later I'll forget about those stupid comments I read."

I nodded. "Okay. Good. Just let me know if you ever want to try again."

We cleared away the remains of our lunch and went to sit by the pool. Luis waved from his perch, and the girls and I waved back. I whispered to Mia. "What? No swimming lessons today?"

She sighed. "Luis and I talked it out. He said we're better off being friends, since he felt like he could never really trust me again, and he couldn't go out with someone he didn't completely trust."

"Wow," I said. "Brutally honest."

"Yeah. Honesty is a big thing for him. I guess it is for me now too. I learned my lesson," Mia said sadly.

"Well, he's still a nice friend to have," I said.

"Mmm–hmm," she agreed. "But do you want to know the worst part?"

"Not really," joked Katie.

Mia smiled. "Now he's dating a girl from the swim team."

"No!" said Katie.

"So you mean, if you'd just been yourself and let him see what a great swimmer you were from the get-go, he could be your boyfriend right now?" I asked incredulously.

"Yup!" said Mia, standing up. "Can you believe it? I really messed up that one."

"Well, live and learn," I said.

A few weeks later, I received an e-mail from Lindsay Miller. It said:

> Emma,
>
> Check out the ad campaign (link below). It's awesome! Thank you so much! And check your e-mail soon for an invitation to something fun from us!

I immediately clicked on the ad's link, and my browser opened to a series of amazing shots of me mixing cupcake batter, frosting cupcakes, decorating them, and more. Victor had used a soft, gauzy lens with diffused lighting so nothing was sharp or harsh. He hadn't really shot the photos directly of my face, either. Instead, most of the pictures were from the side or above, so you saw hints of me but not all of me. They were really, really pretty, and the pink-and-white color scheme turned out beautifully.

I clicked on the link for the group shots and was again dazzled by what a great job Victor had done. Despite his occasionally cranky attitude, the guy was seriously talented. And my friends looked awesome! They would be thrilled.

Quickly, I forwarded the e-mail to the Cupcakers and to my parents.

I almost uploaded it right to social media, but thank goodness I realized just in time what a mistake that would be. The Cupcakers looked pretty in the shots, but surely there would always be trolls out there, and I didn't need to put anyone through all that again.

Katie was still mildly traumatized and had turned down an invitation to do a bridal fashion show with me at A Special Day bridal salon. She had said that modeling was just not for her, and I respected that, even as I told Katie that Mona had seen her ad and thought she was "divine!" ("Divine" was Mona's highest compliment.)

The Cupcakers and my parents all loved the Three Sisters campaign, especially because it was about the cupcakes first and us second. Plus, the photos were gorgeous, and none of them focused too intently on any one of us. We looked busy and happy and un-self-conscious in the shots, which I am sure is part of what made them so pretty.

A few days later, an e-vite arrived in all our in-boxes. We were invited to the launch of the Three Sisters campaign-and-franchise roll-out party at the same loft in SoHo where we'd had the photo shoot.

None of us hesitated: We wanted to go!

My mom offered to chaperone us, and when the day came, we got ready together at my house before we left for the city.

Mia had styled each of us, telling us what to bring from our wardrobe. She had a satchel of accessories to try on us all. Everyone came with wet hair and took turns primping in my bathroom, curling their hair and trying on some of my very basic makeup.

As we left, my dad took a photo. "Wow, girls. Watch out, city! You're going to break some hearts tonight!"

"Oh, Dad!" I rolled my eyes, but he knew I loved the teasing.

Everyone from the campaign was at the party in the loft. The ad agency lady was so thrilled with the results (she'd gotten a promotion and raise because of it) that she dragged us around to meet everyone at the event. When we reached Victor, he kissed us all theatrically and introduced us to a bigwig modeling agent with whom he was chatting.

"You, I know. Gorgeous!" she said to me. Then she cocked her head and looked at Katie. "Don't I recognize you from somewhere?" she said.

"I discovered her! I did her first shoot!" said Victor, putting his arm around her possessively.

Oh brother, I thought. *Now suddenly you're her best friend.*

But the agent was wagging a finger at Katie. "Were you in Paris in the spring? I'm sure I know you from the catwalk."

"Um, no?" said Katie, turning beet red. "I just did a coat campaign for a national coat brand, though."

"Here's my card," said the agent. "Do you have representation?"

"No?" said Katie, smiling awkwardly.

"Call me," said the woman firmly, and she grabbed Victor's arm and led him away to the bar.

"See, Katie? You never know where your next opportunity will come from. That's what I always say!" said Alexis. "Be prepared!"

"There's only one model here," Katie said pointedly. "And that's Emma."

"Models or not, we're all awesome!" I said. "Whether we're modeling on a catwalk or baking cupcakes."

"Here's to us!" Alexis cheered, holding up a cupcake. "The Cupcake Girls—stars wherever we go, whatever we do!"

"To the Cupcake Girls!" Mia agreed. "And to catwalks and cupcakes!" And we all laughed as we clinked our cupcakes together. Cheers!

Here's a small taste
of the very first book in the

series written by Coco Simon:

SUNDAY
SUNDAES

PLOT TWIST

A hot August wind lifted my brown hair and cooled the back of my neck as I waited for the bus to take me to my new school. I hoped I was standing in the right spot. I hoped I was wearing the right thing. I wished I were anywhere else.

My toes curled in my new shoes as I reached into my messenger bag and ran my thumb along the worn spine of my favorite book. I'd packed *Anne of Green Gables* as a good-luck charm for my first day at my new school. The heroine, Anne Shirley, had always cracked me up and given me courage. To me, having a book around was like having an old friend for company. And, boy, did I need a friend right about now.

Ten days before, I'd returned from summer

camp to find my home life completely rearranged. It hadn't been obvious at first, which was almost worse. The changes had come out in drips, and then all at once, leaving me standing in a puddle in the end.

My mom and dad picked me up after seven glorious weeks of camp up north, where the temperature is cool and the air is sweet and fresh. I was excited to get home, but as soon as I arrived, I missed camp. Camp was fun, and freedom, and not really worrying about anything. There was no homework, no parents, and no little brothers changing the ringtone on your phone so that it plays only fart noises. At camp this year I swam the mile for the first time, and all my camp besties were there. My parents wrote often: cheerful e-mails, mostly about my eight-year-old brother, Tanner, and the funny things he was doing. When they visited on Parents' Weekend, I was never really alone with them, so the conversation was light and breezy, just like the weather.

The ride home was normal at first, but I noticed my parents exchanging glances a couple of times, almost like they were nervous. They looked different too. My dad seemed more muscular and was tan, and my mom had let her hair—dark brown and wavy, like mine—grow longer, and it made her look younger. The minute I got home, I grabbed my sweet cat, Diana (named after Anne Shirley's best friend, naturally), and scrambled into my room. Sharing a bunkhouse with eleven other girls for a summer was great, but I was really glad to be back in my own quiet room. I texted SHE'S BAAAACK! to my best friends, Tamiko Sato and Sierra Perez, and then took a really long, hot shower.

It wasn't until dinnertime that things officially got weird.

"You must've really missed me," I said as I sat down at the kitchen table. They'd made all of my favorites: meat lasagna, garlic bread, and green salad with Italian dressing and cracked pepper. It was the meal we always had the night before I left for camp and the night I got back. My mouth started watering.

I grinned as I put my napkin onto my lap.

"We *did* miss you, Allie!" said my mom brightly.

"They talked about you all the time," said Tanner, rolling his eyes and talking with his mouth full of garlic bread, his dinner napkin still sitting prominently on the table.

"Napkin on lapkin!" I scolded him.

"Boys don't use napkins. That's what sleeves are

for," said Tanner, smearing his buttery chin across the shoulder of his T-shirt.

"Gross!" Coming out of the all-girl bubble of camp, I had forgotten the rougher parts of the boy world. I looked to my parents to reprimand him, but they both seemed lost in thought. "Mom? Dad? Hello? Are you okay with this?" I asked, looking to both of them for backup.

"Hmm? Oh, Tanner, don't be disgusting. Use a napkin," said my mom, but without much feeling behind it.

He smirked at me, and when she looked away, he quickly wiped his chin on his sleeve again. It was like all the rules had flown out the window since I'd been gone!

My dad cleared his throat in the way he usually did when he was nervous, like when he had to practice for a big sales presentation. I looked up at him; he was looking at my mom with his eyebrows raised. His bright blue eyes—identical to mine—were *definitely* nervous.

"What's up?" I asked, the hair on my neck prickling a little. When there's tension around, or sadness, I can always feel it. It's not like I'm psychic or anything. I can just feel people's feelings coming off them in waves. Maybe my parents' fighting as I was growing up had made me sensitive to stuff, or maybe it was from reading so many books and feeling the characters' feelings along with them. Whatever it was, my mom said I had a lot of empathy. And right now my empathy meter was registering *high alert*.

My mom swallowed hard and put on a sunny smile that was a little too bright. Now I was really suspicious. I glanced at Tanner, but he was busy dragging a slab of garlic bread through the sauce from his second helping of lasagna.

"Allie, there's something Dad and I would like to tell you. We've made some new plans, and we're pretty excited about them."

I looked back and forth between the two of them. What she was saying didn't match up with the anxious expressions on their faces.

"They're getting divorced," said Tanner through a mouthful of lasagna and bread.

"What?" I said, shocked, but also . . . kind of not. I felt a huge sinking in my stomach, and tears pricked my eyes. I knew there had been more fighting than usual before I'd left for camp, but I hadn't really seen this coming. Or maybe I had; it was like divorce had been there for a while, just slightly to the side of everything, riding shotgun all along. Automatically my brain raced through the list of

book characters whose parents were divorced: Mia in the Cupcake Diaries, Leigh Botts in *Dear Mr. Henshaw*, Karen Newman in *It's Not the End of the World*. . . .

My mother sighed in exasperation at Tanner.

"Wait, Tanner knew this whole time and I didn't?" I asked.

"Sweetheart," said my dad, looking at me kindly. "This has been happening this summer, and since Tanner was home with us, he found out about it first." Tanner smirked at me, but Dad gave him a look. "I know this is hard, but it's actually really happy news for me and your mom. We love each other very much and will stay close as a family."

"We're just tired of all the arguing. And we're sure you two are too. We feel that if we live apart, we'll be happier. All of us."

My mind raced with questions, but all that came out was, "What about me and Tanner? And Diana? Where are we going to live?"

"Well, I found a great apartment right next to the playground," said my dad, suddenly looking happy for real. "You know that new converted factory building over in Maple Grove, with the rooftop pool that we always talk about when we pass by?"

"And I've found a really great little vintage

house in Bayville. And you won't believe it, but it's right near the beach!"

I stared at them.

Mom swallowed hard and kept talking. "It's just been totally redone, and the room that will be yours has built-in bookcases all around it and a window seat," she said.

"And it has a hot tub," added my dad.

"Right," laughed my mom. "And there are plantings in the flower beds around the house, so we can have fresh flowers all spring, summer, and fall!" My mom loved flowers, but my dad grew up doing so much yard work for his parents that he refused to ever let her plant anything here. The house did sound nice, but then something occurred to me.

"Wait, Bayville and Maple Grove? So what about school?" Bayville was ten minutes away!

"Well." My parents shared a pleased look as my mom spoke. "Since my new house is in Bayville, you qualify for seventh grade at the Vista Green School! It's the top-rated school in the district, and it's gorgeous! Everything was newly built just last year. Tan will go to MacBride Elementary."

"Isn't that great?" said my dad.

"Um, *what*? We're changing *schools*?" The lasagna was growing cold on my plate, but how could I eat?

I looked at Tanner to see how he was reacting to all this news, but he was nearly finished with his second helping of lasagna and showed no sign of stopping. The shoulder of his T-shirt now had red sauce stains smeared across it. I looked back at my mom.

"Yes, sweetheart. I know it will be a big transition at first. Everything is going to be new for us all! A fresh start!" said my mom enthusiastically.

Divorce. Moving. A new school.

"Is there any *more* news?" I asked, picking at a crispy corner of my garlic bread.

"Actually," my mom began, looking to my dad, "I have some really great news. Dad and I decided it probably wasn't a good idea for me to go on being the chief financial officer of his company. So I've rented a space in our new neighborhood, and . . . I'm opening an ice cream store, just like I've always dreamed! Ta-da!" She threw her arms wide and grinned.

My jaw dropped as I lifted my head in surprise. "Really?" My mom made the best—I mean the absolute *best*—homemade ice cream in the world. She made a really thick, creamy ice cream base, and then she was willing to throw in anything for flavor: lemon and blueberries, crumbled coffee cake, crushed candy canes, you name it. She was known for her ice cream. I mean, people came to our house and actually asked if she had any in the freezer.

My mom was nodding vigorously, the smile huge on her face. She looked happier and younger than I'd seen her in years. And my dad looked happier than he had in a long time.

"And you two can be the taste testers!" said my mom.

"Yessss!" said Tanner, pumping his fist out and back against his chest. "And our friends, too?" he asked.

"Yes. All of your friends can test flavors too," said my mom.

"Okay, wait." I couldn't take this all in at once. It felt like someone had removed my life and replaced it with a completely new version.

Who were these people? What was my family? *Who was I?*

"Eat your dinner, honey," urged my dad. "It's your favorite. There's plenty of time to talk through all of this."

My eyes suddenly brimmed with tears; I just couldn't help it. Even if—and this was a big "if" for me—this would be a good move for our family, there was still a new house and a new *school*. What about my friends? What about Book Fest, the reading celebration at my school that I helped organize and was set to run this year?

I wiped my eyes with my sleeve. "What about Book Fest?" I said meekly.

My mom stood and came around to hug me. "Oh, Allie, I'm sure they'll still let you come."

I pulled away. "Come? I *run* it! Who's going to run it now? And what will I do instead?"

I scraped my chair away from the table, pulled away from my mom, and raced to my room. Diana was curled up on my bed, and she jumped when I closed the door hard behind me. (It wasn't a slam, but almost.) I grabbed Diana, flopped onto the bed, and had a good cry. Certainly Anne Shirley would have thrown herself onto her bed and cried, at least at first. But what would Hermione Granger have done? Violet Baudelaire? Katniss Everdeen? My favorite characters encountered a lot of troubles, but they usually got through them okay, and it wasn't by lying around crying about them. I sniffed and reached for a tissue, and slid up against my headboard into a sitting position so that I could have a good think, like a plot analysis.

My parents had been unhappy for a long time. I kind of knew that. I mean, I guess we were all unhappy because Mom and Dad fought a lot.

They both worked hard at their jobs, and I knew they were tired, so I always thought a lot of it was just crankiness. Plus Mom was the business manager and my dad ran the marketing group at their company, so I figured since they worked together all day, they just got on each other's nerves after work. But if I really thought about it, I realized that they were like that on the weekends, and even on holidays and vacations. They snapped at each other. They rolled their eyes. And sometimes one of them stomped out of the room. And the more I thought about it, I realized they hadn't spent a lot of time together over the past year. Either Mom would be taking me to soccer and Dad would be staying home with Tanner, or Dad would be doing carpool and errands while Mom went with Tanner to his music lessons. We always ate dinner together, but starting last winter and right up to when I'd left for camp, there had been a lot of pretty quiet meals, with each of us lost in our own thoughts. Mom would talk to me or to Tanner, and Dad would always ask about our days, but they never actually spoke to each other.

I squeezed my eyes shut and tried to think of the last time we'd all been happy together. The night before I left for camp, maybe? We had my favorite dinner, and Dad was teasing that it would be the last great meal before I ate camp food for the summer. Mom joked that we should sneak some lasagna into my shoes, which Tanner thought was a really good idea. Dad ran and picked up one of my sneakers, and Mom pretended to spoon some in. We were being silly and laughing, and I felt warm and snug and cozy. I loved camp and couldn't wait to go every year, but I remembered thinking right then that I'd miss being at the table with my family around me.

Later that night, though, I heard Mom and Dad fighting about something in their room, like they seemed to do almost every night. Then for seven weeks I went to sleep hearing crickets and giggles instead of angry whispers, along with a few warnings of "Girls, it's time to go to bed!" from my counselors.

Now I heard whispers from Mom and Dad on the other side of the door. They weren't angry, but they didn't sound happy, either. Then I heard the whispers fade as they went downstairs.

I guess I fell asleep, because when I woke up, Dad was sitting on my bed and Mom was standing next to him, looking worried. The lights were out, but my room was bright from the moon.

"Allie," Dad said gently. "You need to brush your teeth and get ready for bed."

"Do you want to talk about anything?" Mom asked as I sat up.

Suddenly I was really annoyed. "Oh, you mean like how you decided to get a divorce and not tell me? Or sell our house and not tell me? Or that I would need to move schools and totally start over again? Nope, nothing to discuss at all." I crossed my arms over my chest.

"Allie," Mom said, and her voice broke. I could tell she was upset, but I didn't care. "We are divorcing because we think it will make us happier. All of us."

"Speak for yourself," I said. I knew I was being mean, and on any usual day one of them would tell me to watch my tone.

"It is going to be hard," said Dad slowly. "It's going to be an adjustment, and it's going to take a lot of patience from all of us. We are not sugarcoating that part. But it's going to be better. You and Tanner mean everything to us, and Mom and I are going to do what will make you happiest. This separation will make us stronger as a family. Things will be better, and we need you to believe that."

"And what if I don't?" I said. I knew I was on thin ice. Even I could tell that I sounded a little bratty. "What will make me happiest is to stay in this house and go to the same school with my friends and . . ." I thought about it for a second. "Wait, if I'm moving to Bayville, when will I ever see Dad?"

"A lot still needs to be worked out," said Mom. "For now you and Tanner and Diana will live with me at the house in Bayville during the week. Dad will come over every Wednesday, and every other weekend you'll be at Dad's apartment in Maple Grove."

I looked at Dad. "So every other week I'll only see you on Wednesdays?" I felt my eyes filling with tears again.

"We can work things out, Allie," said Dad quickly. "I am still here and I am still your dad and I will always be around."

"I promise you, Allie, we're going to do everything we can to make this better for all of us," Mom said. I couldn't see her face clearly, but I could see that she was trying hard not to cry.

Dad reached over and gave Mom's arm a little squeeze. I sat there looking at them, not being able to remember the last time I'd seen Mom give Dad a kiss hello, or Dad hug Mom. Now here they were, but even that didn't seem right.

"I'm not brushing my teeth," I said. I don't really know why I said that. I guess I just wanted to feel like I was still in control of something, anything. Then I turned away from them and pulled up the covers. All I wanted to do was go to sleep, because I was really hoping I would wake up and this would all be a bad dream.

I woke up and blinked a few times, remembering that I was back in my room at home and not still at camp. Well, home for now.

I slowly got up and listened at the door. I could hear Mom talking and the *clink* of a spoon in a bowl, which meant Tanner was slurping his cereal. I didn't want to stay in my room, but I didn't want to go downstairs either. I grabbed my phone. With all of the drama the night before, I had completely forgotten to check it. I looked at the screen, and there were eighteen messages, ranging from did a big scary monster eat you???? to OMG she came back and now she's gone again! from my best friends, Tamiko and Sierra. I sent a couple of quick texts to them, and within seconds my phone was buzzing, as I'd known it would be.

Just then Mom knocked at my door and opened it. "Good morning, sweetie!" she said with her new Sally Sunshine voice that I was already not liking. "I'm so glad to have my girl home!"

I looked at her. Was she just going to pretend nothing had happened?

Mom came in and sat down on my bed. "Dad left for work, but I took this week off. The movers are coming in a couple of days, and we'll need time to settle into our new house." She looked at me. I stared at the wall. The wall of my room, where I had lived since I was a baby. I looked at the spot behind the door, and Mom followed my eyes. She sighed. Since I had been tiny, Dad had measured me on the wall on my birthday and had made a little mark at the top of my head. He'd even done it last year, even though I'd told him I was way too old. "I'm going to miss this house," she said softly. "It has a lot of memories."

It was quiet for a second. Mom looked like she was far away.

"You took your first steps in the kitchen," she said, really smiling this time. "And remember your seventh birthday party that we had in the backyard?" I did. It was a fairy tea party, and each kid got fairy wings and a magic wand. There had been so many birthdays and holidays in this house.

I had never lived in another house. All I knew was this one. I knew that there were thirty-eight steps between the front porch and the bus stop. I could run up the stairs to the second floor in eight seconds (Tanner and I had timed each other), and I knew that the cabinet door in the kitchen where we kept the cookies creaked when you opened it.

"I think you'll like the new house," said Mom. "Houses. You'll have two homes."

I looked straight ahead.

"Your new room has bookcases all around it. I thought of you when I saw it and knew you would love it." Mom looked at me. "And there's a really great backyard to hang out in. I'm thinking about getting a hammock maybe, and definitely some comfy rocking chairs."

"What about my new other house?" I asked.

"Well," Mom said, "Dad's house is an apartment, actually, and it has really cool views. It's modern, and my house is more old-fashioned. It's the best of both worlds!"

I sighed.

Mom sighed. "Honey, I know this is tough."

I still didn't answer. Mom stood up.

"Well, kiddo, we have a lot to do. I'm guessing

Tamiko and Sierra are coming over soon?"

I looked at my phone lighting up. "Maybe," I said.

Mom nodded. "Okay. Well, let me know what you want to do today. It's your first day back. Tomorrow, though, we do need to pack up your room. Dad and I have been packing things up for the past few weeks, but there's still a lot to do."

I looked into the hall. I must have missed the fact that there were some boxes stacked there. One was marked "Mom" and one was marked "Dad."

Mom followed my gaze. "We're trying to make sure there are familiar things in each house. You can split up your room or . . . I was thinking maybe you'd like to get a new bedroom set?" There was that fake bright happy voice again.

I looked around the room. I liked my room. If the house couldn't stay the same, at least my room could. "No," I said. "I want this stuff."

"We should also talk about your new school," Mom said.

I looked down at my feet. My toenails were painted in my camp colors, blue and yellow. I wiggled them.

"You're already enrolled, but I talked to the principal about having you come over to take a tour and maybe meet some of your new teachers."

I shrugged.

"I think it might be good to take a ride over, just so you are familiar with it before your first day," she said. "It's a bigger school, so you could get the lay of the land. And I've been asking around the new neighborhood, and there are a few girls who will be in your grade."

I nodded.

"Okay," she said brightly. "Well, we have this week to do that, so we'll just find a good time to go."

I swallowed hard.

Mom stood in the doorway and waited a minute, then stepped back into the room quickly, gathered me up in her arms, and hugged me tightly. "It's going to be better, baby girl," she said, kissing the top of my head like she used to when I was little. She was using her normal voice again. "I promise you, it might be hard, but it's definitely going to be better."

I tried really, really hard not to cry. A few tears spilled out, and Mom wiped them away. She took my face in her hands and looked at me. "Now," she said, "first things first, because I think there's a griddle that's calling our names."

I knew the tradition, so I had to smile.

"Welcome-back pancakes!" we said at the same time. Mom's blueberry pancakes were my welcome-home-from-camp tradition. She always put ice cream on them to make them into smiley faces and wrote "XO" in syrup on my plate. I could already taste them. I stood up and followed Mom downstairs. Maybe she was right about things. This day was already getting a little bit better.

The next couple of days were a blur. On our last night in the house, we sat on the grass in the backyard. We had been packing and hauling boxes, and we were all sweaty and dirty and tired. Mom and Dad had emptied out the refrigerator and cabinets, so we had kind of a mishmash to eat. Tanner was eating cereal, peanut butter, crackers, and a hot dog that Dad had made on the grill. For dessert Mom pulled out the last carton of ice cream from the freezer, and since we had packed the bowls up, we all stuck spoons in and shared. "Hey!" I yelped as Tanner's spoon jabbed mine.

"I want those chocolate chips!" he said, digging in. Mom laughed. "In about a week we're going to have so much ice cream, we won't even know what to do with it!" Mom's store was opening soon, and since she was so busy with all the details, the packing at home hadn't exactly gone smoothly. Since Mom kept having to go to the store for things like the freezer delivery or to meet with people about things like what kind of spoons to order, we actually got Dad's apartment set up first. It was nice, but it was . . . well, weird. Tanner and I each had our own rooms, but they were kind of small. And Dad's house felt like Dad's, not really like our house. Dad had always loved modern things, so everything was glass and leather. It looked like it should be in a catalog. I was kind of afraid to mess anything up. There were a lot of pictures of me and of Tanner, but the first thing I noticed was that there were no pictures of the four of us.

"Where's the one from New Year's?" I asked, standing in front of a bookcase. We always took a family picture on New Year's Day.

Dad looked around. "Oh," he said, a little flustered. "I guess Mom took those shots. She has more room in the house."

I looked at him. *So this is how it's going to be,* I thought. *The three of us here and the three of us there.*

"We can take some new shots!" Dad said.

"Better," I kept whispering to myself. They'd both promised it was going to be better. But it wasn't really better. It was just downright weird.

The night before moving day, Tanner and I went to bed late. We had been packing all day, and we were beat, but I still couldn't sleep. I heard the back door open. I looked out my window and saw a shadow on the lawn. I almost freaked out, but then I realized that it was Mom, sitting on one of the rocking chairs that we'd bought for the new house but that had accidentally gotten delivered here. She was facing the house, and she looked like she was trying to memorize exactly the way it looked right then. I wondered if she could see me looking out at her. Then I saw Dad walk toward her. It was kind of weird that he was still here, since he had his apartment already, but they had decided that we would all move at the same time. Dad sat down on the grass next to Mom, and I could see them talking but couldn't hear what they were saying. I heard Mom laugh, and then I heard Dad laughing too. It was a nice sound. It was the last night we'd all be sleeping in this house together. I knew we were still a family—they kept telling us that—but it was the last time we'd all live together, and tomorrow morning everything was going to really change. I looked at Mom and Dad laughing, but all it did was make my throat thick. Some things were too sad to see, so I flung myself into bed, hoping I'd fall asleep fast.

When the movers rolled up to the house early the next morning, Mom and Dad had already been up for hours, cleaning and sweeping and taking care of a lot of last-minute stuff. The house already didn't look like ours anymore.

When everything was loaded up, Mom locked the front door and handed Dad the key. We all stood there on the porch for a minute, looking up at the house. *Home.* I started to cry, and so did Mom. I buried my head in Dad's chest, and I could tell he was crying too. Only Tanner, who was sitting on the step playing a game on Dad's phone, seemed unmoved. "Tanner!" I yelled. "Say good-bye to your house!"

Tanner looked up, confused. "Uh, bye, house," he said, and we all laughed.

"Okay, troops," Mom said. "Onward." Tanner and I got into Mom's car, and we pulled out of the driveway. I looked back down our street as long as I could, saying good-bye to everything as it was.

We turned onto the main road, and Mom took a deep breath. "Okay, gang," she said. "On to our next adventure! Here we go."

"To where?" Tanner asked.

"To our new house," Mom said, turning around to look at Tanner. "And to better things ahead."

"Oh," said Tanner. "I thought maybe we were going someplace fun." Mom looked at Tanner like he had ten heads. Then she looked at me, and we both cracked up. Some things, it seemed, weren't going to change at all.